Right Place – Wrong Time

by

Martin Lesley

Dedication

To Valerie,
for her never ending support, good-natured criticism
and selfless understanding of my first foray into writing.

MARTIN LESLEY

Contents

Prologue - 2011

The Easter weekend had been forecast to be one of the best weekends for weather the country had ever known, and for once the forecast was accurate, partly due to Easter being very late this year. For many people, Sunday 24th April will be the latest Easter Day in their lifetimes. Easter Sunday always falls between March 22 and April 25, but the earliest Easter day won't happen again for another 200 years, while the next Easter Sunday on April 25 will not be until 2038.

Easter Saturday morning dawned bright and clear. There was hardly a cloud in the sky. The trees and shrubs were decked in their spring finery, and the birds were singing. There was anticipation that winter had finally gone and spring had arrived. The previous winter had brought heavy snowfalls, record low temperatures, travel chaos and school disruption to the UK, with the coldest December since records began in 1910, and thought to have been the coldest since before 1659.

The fine weather had brought families out into Holland Park, and covering 22 hectares was the largest park in the Royal Borough of Kensington and Chelsea. They were looking forward to enjoying the sunshine and adventure provided by the many amenities, including the parks roaming muster of peacocks and the magnificent Japanese Kyoto Garden, donated by the Kyoto Chamber of Commerce in 1991. An oasis of peace and tranquillity the garden was filled with Japanese maple and cherry trees and has the famous tiered waterfall which trickles into the koi carp filled pond.

Stephanie and Klara had walked from their home in nearby Phillimore Place, with Emilie the French au pair. Klara's father

Marcus had wanted to have a German au pair, but Stephanie had insisted on French, as it would be good for Klara to regularly speak another language. Marcus had agreed, with the proviso that she could also speak German fluently. He had intervened in the interview and had quizzed her in German. Emilie had passed with flying colours, having studied German at school and university. Marcus was suitably impressed and approved of Stephanie's decision to hire her. Stephanie was dressed in a pale green flowery dress with short sleeves and a white shrug and was wearing her latest acquisition, a pair of Jimmy Choo white sandals. Stephanie had recently taken to wearing Jimmy Choo shoes, finding them both comfortable and the height of fashion. Emilie, although still very fashionable, was more conservatively dressed in navy cropped trousers with a white blouse, navy and white striped cardigan and casual navy loafers, Klara, in a cute cream t-shirt and navy shorts with ankle socks and sandals, insisted on seeing both the peacocks and the koi carp. The trio wandered around the park enjoying the spring sunshine.

Stephanie herself could speak several languages, having been born and raised in Germany until she was fourteen, then moving to America, where she had met and married Marcus. Marcus had been called into the embassy earlier in the morning, to deal with some diplomatic emergency, and was still finding his feet after having been appointed German Ambassador to the United Kingdom four months earlier, by Chancellor Angela Merkel. In November, dressed in a grey morning suit, crisp white shirt with grey silk tie and carrying matching top hat and gloves, he was accompanied by Stephanie, wearing Donatella Versace and Phillip Treacy creations, and attended Buckingham Palace in a ceremony that would live in their memories forever. The equerry announced "The German Ambassador Marcus and Mrs Stephanie Meier," They walked nervously up to the Queen, who was dressed in a pale blue dress with matching shoes and wearing the insignia of a Knight of the Garter, Marcus, towering over the Queen, bowed, Stephanie made a deep curtsey, and Marcus handed over his credentials as the German Ambassador to the Court of St James. The Queen congratulated Marcus on his appointment and welcomed him to England. She asked Stephanie about their family, and Stephanie told her proudly about their daughter Klara. They chatted for several minutes more before they took their leave with a bow and small curtsey again. Returning to the German Embassy, Marcus and Stephanie hosted a cocktail party for the staff, also inviting the British Prime Minister, Foreign Secretary, Home Secretary and many of the senior Foreign and Home Office officials. Stephanie was very nervous but carried off her duties as hostess with apparent ease and grace.

The family had purchased their five storey Victorian house three months ago, and Stephanie was busy transforming its dated interior decor into a bright and airy modern look. Workmen had been busy knocking down walls, stripping wallpaper and paint, rewiring electrics, refitting bathrooms, a sumptuous fitted kitchen, and re-plastering walls and ceilings for several weeks and had completed the redecorations to all of the first three floors. Whilst the renovations were in progress, they had stayed at The Savoy, but now that there was only the top floor and basement left to receive the makeover, they had finally moved in. Marcus wanted a cinema in the basement, and extensive soundproofing had been installed in the basement ceiling space and dividing walls. Phillimore Place was one of several streets making up the area of Holland Park, having been acquired in the 1770's by Lord Holland for £17,000, about £2.3 million today and the area was considered to be one of the most desirable in the Royal Borough.

Once Klara had seen the Koi carp and the peacocks she had happily played nearby whilst Stephanie and Emilie were content to sit in the sunshine chatting about a forthcoming diplomatic cocktail party. Klara had joined several children at the various items of play equipment and was currently riding on a roundabout. Three or four boys riding bicycles had left their bikes lying by the side of the roundabout and we're jumping on and off whilst pushing it faster and faster.

A scream cut through the pleasant morning air, silencing the noisy playground. Mothers sitting together on park benches gossiping, looked to see if it was their child. Children, who had been playing happily, anxiously looked around for their mothers. A child, a girl of around 8 years of age, was lying in a crumpled heap beside one of the bicycles, lying on the ground at the side of the still spinning roundabout. Four boys, looking shocked, were standing around the roundabout they had been spinning as fast as they could.

For what seemed an eternity the scene resembled a still photograph, then all of a sudden, movement returned. Emilie ran from her seat to the fallen girl, Klara. The boys grabbed their bicycles and sped off. Klara was blonde, with a pigtail neatly tied with a red ribbon, and now had the accessory of blood from a rather large gash to her head, the stain spreading onto her cream tee shirt. Emilie bent over Klara, whose left-arm was at a rather strange angle, pulled her mobile from the pocket of her navy jacket, and pressed speed dial 2 for the Embassy.
"Es hat einen Unfall gegeben. Schicken Sie sofort einen Krankenwagen zum Holland Park". (There has been an accident. Send an ambulance immediately to Holland Park).
She gave the location of the playground and then
"Bitte benachrichtigen Sie sofort den Botschafter". (Please notify the Ambassador at once).
Stephanie had sat transfixed on the bench, but got unsteadily to her feet and joined the pair. "I've called for an ambulance Madame and asked the Embassy to notify your husband at once" Emilie told her. Klara was unconscious and Emilie took off her jacket and

wrapped her in it. A few minutes later they could hear the siren growing louder and louder, and the ambulance pulled up outside the playground. Paramedics ran to the child, checked her over, and after immobilising the head and arm, quickly loaded her onto a stretcher.

The women joined Klara in the rear of the ambulance, which then sped along Earls Court Road towards the Chelsea and Westminster Accident Hospital. In the ambulance, Klara had regained consciousness, and was screaming in pain and sobbing uncontrollably. The paramedic was working on the head wound which was bleeding profusely. Her left arm may well be dislocated or even broken. Stephanie sat with clenched fists, her knuckles white, unable to comfort her daughter whilst the paramedics were treating her injuries.
"Da, mein Kleine, Mamas hier wird alles gut", (There my little one, Mummy's here everything will be fine)
she said over and over consoling Klara, and of course, herself. It was to no avail. Understandably, Klara was inconsolable. What Marcus would say when he arrived at the hospital was not worth contemplating. It was sure to be something scathing. At the very least Emilie's position would be untenable.

The ambulance with blue lights and sirens blaring cut a swathe through the oncoming traffic, and pulled up in front of the accident and emergency department doors. The paramedic opened the rear doors of the ambulance, and the driver and the paramedic rushed Klara on the stretcher into A&E. Klara was wheeled into a cubicle with Stephanie and Emilie following close behind. They continued trying to comfort Klara without success. A few minutes later the curtain was pulled back and a junior doctor entered. She was slim, with a pretty face and red hair coiled up into a bun.
"What have we here. There there. Don't worry, I'll look after you. Are you going to be my brave little girl"? At the sound of the

doctor's voice, Klara stopped crying, her eyes opened wide, and stared at the doctor. Stephanie was astonished, and looked at the doctor in surprise.

Yes, thought Klara, she can look after me.

She will look after me.

She DID look after me.

Part I 2005

Chapter 1

Gerry was bursting. If his pride was any greater, he would surely explode. His shift had been arduous, but he had once again been able to deliver all of his packages and get back in time to sort out his route for tomorrow. When he had returned to the warehouse, Mr Johannsson, his manager, had called him into his office. "Gerry, you can take the new van out tomorrow", slapped him on the back, and set off for home, looking over his shoulder chuckling, and said, "Mind you don't scratch it".

Gerry had stayed late last night, for well over an hour, looking all over the new Mercedes Sprinter 3.5t medium wheelbase van, with a 129 bhp 2.1 litre engine, automatic transmission and cruise control, it was resplendent in its brown and gold UPS livery. He had sat behind the wheel, adjusting the driver's seat several times before finally settling on the right position. Made sure the wing mirrors were correctly positioned, checked where all of the controls were located, made sure the doors opened, closed and locked properly, slid the windows up and down, and checked the odometer, 17 km. He even read the manual, well, some of it anyway. He opened the bonnet, looked at the engine, gleaming, without any road dirt. Satisfied, he found where he could put his flask and sandwiches and hang his winters coat. He was just like a child in a sweet shop.

When he eventually left, he could not stop grinning. His girlfriend Madeline would be so happy for him. His punctuality and smartness had paid off, and now he was the first in the depot to drive the new van and he hoped he would be able to drive it permanently. He promised himself he would be there in good time tomorrow to collect the cherished vehicle, loaded with his deliveries, and would have the best day of his life.

Gerry had come to France from Tunisia at 17, leaving behind his father, mother and two sisters. His father owned a stall in the souk in Akouda just outside Port El Kantaoui, and was disappointed that his son would not follow him into his business, eventually taking over, but Gerry was adamant that he wanted to make his own way in the world. He did not intend to be another souk worker or beach salesman selling sunglasses and handbags to the tourists like many of his countrymen, but wanted to fashion out a proper career for himself. He was quiet and polite, tall and slim, , smart and quite handsome. He had been a good student at school, excelling in languages. As well as his native Arabic, he spoke fluent French, very good English, and passable German and Italian. He could drive, although he had not passed any test, but was used to driving the buggies at El Kantaoui golf club, where he had caddied for several years. He had driven his father's old van around the back streets of Akouda since he was 10 years old, sitting on a cushion to see through the windscreen, helping to deliver goods from the souk. He had saved hard for when he would move to France, and would be 18 in five months' time, so he intended to follow a career as a driver of some sorts. He fell on his feet within six days of landing in Marseilles, seeing an advert for a warehouseman with UPS, and thought that if he worked hard there, he could move on to be a delivery driver when he passed his driving test. He found a small flat in a tower block not far from the sea front.

Gerry worked hard as a warehouseman, and when he was eighteen, he passed his driving test at the first attempt. He then started pestering his manager to let him start driving, but the manager was adamant that he had to remain in the warehouse. For several months Gerry remained patient, but eventually he was allowed to go out on deliveries as an assistant to the driver. He was very keen and willing to learn, and watched everything the driver did with the paperwork. Shortly after, he got his big break. A driver in Lyon had been taken ill and they were looking for a replacement. Gerry jumped at the chance and left Marseille's and arrived in Lyon to start as a driver. His experience in riding as assistant to the driver proved invaluable, and he settled into his new role comfortably. It was not long after he arrived in Lyon that he met his girlfriend, Madeleine. She was from a small village outside Reims and was in her first year studying journalism at the Universite de Lyon. She was stunningly attractive with short dark hair cut in a chic gamine style. She had high cheekbones and large brown eyes which would melt his heart on a regular basis. He could not believe how lucky he had been to meet her. After only a few short months she had moved into his flat, to save money for the rent of course, and he had never been happier in his life.

On his way home he thought about his day tomorrow. He also hoped he would be able to complete his deliveries on time, as the second love of his life, Liverpool FC, were through to the knockout stage of the European Champions League, and were playing the German side Bayer Leverkusen that night in the round of 16. The match was being broadcast on TV and he didn't want to miss that and hoped to see his hero, Steven Gerrard, score the winning goal. Bayer Leverkusen had finished third in the Bundesliga the previous season, and had qualified to start this competition in the third qualifying round. They had then progressed through the group stage by winning group B on goal difference from Real Madrid. No mean feat, as Real were the most successful side in European competition history.

Liverpool had not tasted European success since 1985, and he had never followed his team through this competition. Liverpool had been banned from European competition for six years, following the 1985 Heysel disaster, in which 32 Italian fans and 7 others had died. Juventus had won that final 1 nil, and it saw the end of Liverpool's dominance of European competition, having collected seven trophies in eleven years. Four years later, fourteen Liverpool fans were jailed for manslaughter. Now, hopefully, there would be a more peaceful return to the big time.

Chapter 2

Alexsander (Alex) was from Gdansk, and had the same work ethic as his father and grandfather before him. Always be punctual, smart and polite. It had served him well. He had risen from being a taxi driver to chauffeur one of Germany's prominent industrialists.

Alex's mother had died when he was 9, and he became angry and a little wild, getting into many scrapes with the local police. Since his first joyride at the age of 12, he had been car crazy, and his father had recognised his sons need to have something positive in his life, so had encouraged his love of driving. He had worked overtime in the shipyards of Gdansk to raise the money to buy an old car, and took Alex out into the fields outside of Gdansk, taught him to drive, and how to maintain and look after the car. Alex had also worked hard in the small garage at the end of the street where he lived, watching the mechanics, helping them repair the cars, then washing and cleaning them for collection by their owners. He put away any tips the customers gave him, towards his ultimate goal of passing his driving test.

On his eighteenth birthday he applied for his licence. It is a costly business in Poland, consisting first of a £40 medical examination, then 30 hours of theoretical lectures, followed by 30 hours of practical driving, at a cost of £200. The examinations were another £35, so it was not cheap. It was just as well that Alex had saved hard.

On passing his test he started work driving for a delivery company, and in his spare time, a mini bus for a local charity. After having gained a years' experience he became a taxi driver. The hours were long, but with tips his earnings increased drastically, bringing his ambition that much nearer. He wanted to become a chauffeur, but not just any chauffeur, a chauffeur with all the necessary protection skills needed to work for high profile clients. After three years he had saved enough money to go on an evasive driving course, which included anti kidnap, protection survival and abduction management. He passed with flying colours.

His first chauffeurs' job was for the chairman of the Gdansk shipping yard, who had lost his licence after what he considered a small indiscretion, in having too much alcohol in the blood, following the launch of another ship. After this period of suspension was over, Alex was looking for other employment. Gdansk, he felt, was too small, so he travelled into Germany looking for other opportunities. His credentials were impeccable, and it was not long before he secured his dream position with the CEO of a pharmaceutical company. He had held this job now for two years, and was very content with his life. He drove very expensive cars, to very expensive places, and his down time was also very rewarding. A little side line was earning him a very nice nest egg thank you. Nobody notices you when you are driving an important person between countries.

Alex was handsome, even though he said it himself. He wasn't vain, but the girls all seemed to fall over themselves for his attention. He was tall, at least 6 feet, maybe 6'1" and had dark wavy hair that cascaded over his brow when he removed his chauffeurs cap. He had brown eyes, high cheekbones, square jaw, a good tanned complexion, and worked out regularly using the gym at his chauffeurs flat, giving him a good physique. There was also the fringe benefit of the nannies. They changed quite regularly, so it did not matter to him that they moved on, or were moved on. Saved him the embarrassment of ending the relationship. He hadn't fathered a child yet, at least not that he was aware of. The current nanny was Isabella, from the UK, probably Chelsea or Belgravia, or somewhere similar going by her accent.

Isabella was young, probably 19 or so, and was perfectly groomed. She had been the current nanny for six weeks, and had already fallen for Alex's good looks. When he had picked her up at Geneva airport, in the first week of the new year, he immediately sensed the chemistry between them. He was sure she would be another easy acquisition.

Isabella Violet Francine. Isabella, Izzy, as she preferred to be known, was an only child, and the centre of her family's attention. It had taken years of perseverance before she had finally come into the world by the miracle of IVF, which provided the inspiration for her Christian names. Her father was a successful barrister, and no expense had been spared, showering his only child with every material benefit, in addition to her parents overwhelming love. As well as being extremely clever, she was a very pretty girl, slim with long blonde hair in a pony tail and the typical English rose complexion. Educated at private schools, she was also an accomplished rider, winning many rosettes at gymkhanas around the family home in Gloucestershire. Summer holidays were spent in the Caribbean, whilst skiing was the family's winter extravagance.

Izzy was now taking a gap year, before going up to Oxford to follow in her father's footsteps and study law. She had spent several months in Africa, volunteering with a charity bringing water to several villages, and had returned home for Christmas. Her father had successfully defended an action against a German pharmaceutical company, and his connections had secured Izzy a position with the CEO's family, so in the first week of January she flew off to Germany to begin life as a nanny. Although Izzy had no brothers and sisters, she adored children, having several cousins she had played with, and babysat during her teenage years.

She immediately fell in love with Klara when they met. Klara was nearly three, going on 18, and was a lively inquisitive little girl, fair hair, blue eyes and bright rosy cheeks, she was the image of her mother Stephanie. Izzy liked Stephanie, but felt uncomfortable under the stern gaze of her father Marcus. Izzy tried to remember the games she used to play with her cousins, and was trying hard to bond with Klara. She felt she was making progress and Klara could be very affectionate, but also had a tenancy to sulk. Izzy soon developed a routine for getting up early and dressing Klara, before making breakfast for them both.

When he had collected her from the airport in Geneva, six weeks ago, her heart had skipped a beat, and she looked forward to every minute spent with him. She had flirted with him outrageously, demure one minute, provocative the next, and was sure he was responding to her charms.

Chapter 3

Daniel Hodge wasn't particularly a looker. He wasn't very tall, 5 foot 9 or so, with fair hair and freckles. Bit of a nerd really, but he had a great sense of humour. He could make people laugh. He soon found out that being funny made him popular, and stopped the name calling in his early schooldays. It was also true that having filled out a bit, he had "grown into his face", and was now quite presentable. He was born and bred in East Sussex, and was in his final year studying computer science at Teesside University. He had always been a computer whizz-kid, and it was no surprise when he chose computer science as a degree course. The only surprise was that he had chosen Teesside as his university. The university had gained its 'Excellent' grading for teaching Computer Science under Dean of Computing & Mathematics, Ray Brunskill, who had singled out Daniel as a high flyer, mentoring him and encouraging his development and entrepreneurship. Ray was one of the best-known names in Higher Education Computing, and had set up future Prime Minister Tony Blair's first computer for him. Daniel had read an article about Ray in one of his many computer journals, and that had sealed the deal. Tony Blair had represented the Labour Party in the nearby Sedgefield constituency since 1983, becoming leader of the party in July 1994, and was elected Prime Minister following the Labour Party's landslide victory in the 1997 general election. Blair would go on to be the longest serving Labour Prime Minister and second longest after the Conservative Margaret Thatcher.

Daniels parents were both highly successful in their chosen careers, Dad Barry, being the CEO of a medium sized building company, and Mum Abigail, a chartered accountant and a partner in the KPMG accounting group. In 2001, when Daniel went to Teesside University, they had bought a house in one of Middlesbrough's nicer areas, within easy reach of the university, and this seemed to be the most economically viable solution. The large Victorian terraced building was a house of multiple occupancy, and the rent from three flatmates more than contributed to the cost of the mortgage, although there was still one room empty. The house had needed some refurbishment, and this had been completed in the summer before Daniel took up residence. Daniel used the top floor front two rooms as bedroom and lounge/study area. He was a good student, and had taken to computer programming like a duck to water.

Daniel's grandmother had doted on him, her only grandchild, and when she had passed away just before his going to university, had left him a substantial inheritance. He had discussed his inheritance with his parents, mostly his mother, who with her international accountancy background, advised him to look offshore. She guided him in his research and pointed out the pitfalls and the advantages of the various countries he was looking into. He considered his mums advice and thought he had invested wisely, some of it in a private offshore account in Belize, with the remainder in a High Yield Stocks and Shares savings account in the City of London, and had been very careful not to fritter it away.

Just before the start of his second year, he had had a brainwave. Microsoft, Sony, and Nintendo were fighting it out for control of the high-definition gaming market, with Xbox 360, PlayStation 3, and Wii, battling for supremacy. He had come up with an idea for a new game, and favouring PlayStation 3, was spending most of his time programming the game, hoping that this would set him on the path to becoming a millionaire. He fitted out his study area with a large video screen fixed to the wall and had installed a powerful computer network sufficient for developing his gaming program and his programming skills. This meant many hours coding and debugging, but progress was being made, and he felt it would not be long before his beta version was fully bug free. He was using his flat mates as guinea pigs and they were trying to find the bugs in his software. Then of course would come the hard part. Getting his game accepted and taking it to market.

Daniel may have been a bit of a nerd, but he was a very astute young man and had read many financial journals regarding setting up companies. In one article the writer had extolled the benefits of forming a limited company in Belize because of the high level of privacy both for corporations and individuals. Members of an LLC in Belize don't have to disclose their personal information or financial status in public records. He had also read that there were several advantages to offshore accounts, including the tax benefits, so he thought that it could not be worse than say Barclays or NatWest. This sounded ideal, so Daniel discussed this with his Mum and then registered his company in Belize with himself as Director and Mum, Abigail, as Secretary (not that she would be doing any secretarial work) and opened a company bank account with the Heritage Bank in Belize. He then went back to his keyboard and nights of programming. That was before he met Lizzie.

Lizzie Wells was petite, cute and with long red hair which she currently favoured in a pony tail. Standing at just over 5' 3", she was slim with sparkling green eyes, vivacious, and an infectious giggle which endeared her to all and sundry. She had grown up in the suburbs of Manchester, with her parents, four brothers and a sister, and being the youngest of six children, she had been thoroughly spoilt. Lizzie's father was a foreman in the construction industry, and her mother was a checkout assistant at the local supermarket. After getting 3 A*s in her A Levels at Manchester High School for Girls, Lizzie had enrolled at Newcastle University to study medicine, and was now in her second year. Her parents were overjoyed that Lizzie would be the first member of their family to go to university. Three of her brothers were doing well, Thomas was a plumber, Joseph an electrician, whilst Robert was a self-employed builder carrying out small building works, extensions and modernisations, for private clients. He was lucky that he could call on Tom and Joe for electrical and plumbing works, rather than relying on outside sub-contractors.

The oldest brother Alan, named after his dad, had unfortunately fallen foul of the law, passing on cannabis in a pub to an undercover detective and was currently spending a short spell at Her Majesties pleasure in HM Prison Manchester, formerly Strangeways Prison. The prison had been rebuilt and renamed following a major riot in

1990, reopening in 1994. Despite the rebuilding and modernising works, the prison still records the highest incidence of suicides in the UK prison system. Her sister Margaret, named after her mother, was a carer in a residential home, which she really enjoyed. Lizzie had helped out there during her holidays from school, earning her a little extra pocket money.

Last year she had moved into a flat with three other girls, and had enjoyed her first year at the Teesside satellite department of the university, but was struggling to come to terms with the rather cramped conditions in a run-down area of Stockton. Lizzie had represented her school, the county, and now the university at hockey, and had been called up to a national training camp. She was hoping to represent England at next year's Commonwealth games in Melbourne.

Like most teen-agers she loved her music, and was very loyal to her home town groups, Take That, Elbow, and Oasis, with Liam Gallagher's poster above her bed. She had been devastated when Take That broke up when Robbie Williams had left, but was excited to hear that there was a chance that they were reforming later in the year. Lizzie had seen her idols at several Manchester venues, but preferred the smaller Night People atmosphere. She had had three boyfriends, but nothing serious had developed, and was happy to be a free spirit when she left for university. She was intent on becoming a doctor, and wasn't keen to let love interrupt her career path.

Daniels three flat-mates had been badgering him non-stop to join them at their nightly visit to the local pub, usually without success, but this Friday night, after a particularly fraught session of debugging his program, they had finally persuaded him leave the keyboard and come out for a drink. The guys were in a good mood, the pub had a live band and the place was rocking. Daniel sat quietly enjoying his pints, which were starting to loosen him up and forget all about his programming. The boys noticed a group of girls sitting at a nearby table and went over to chat. That's when he saw Lizzie and was instantly smitten. He was initially tongue-tied, but several drinks, dances and lots of laughs later, he said "Would you like to see the computer game I'm writing?" "At least that's different from would you like to see my etchings," she laughed. They went back to his rooms and while she was trying out the software game, and he made coffee, she said "I'd love to live in a place like this, my room is so cramped," "There is a spare room," he said "why don't you move in," So, she did. The spare room wasn't used a lot.

Meeting Daniel had put a spanner in the works, but Lizzie was adamant that their burgeoning relationship would not distract her from her goal. She loved Daniels dry wit and sense of humour, and they always seemed to be laughing. They were good mates, but she could also not ignore the fact that she was falling in love with him. It was good that he was also obsessed with his computer project, which tied in well with her passion to be a doctor. They both studied hard, but knew how to party when given the opportunity. It was just after Christmas when Daniel suggested they take a complete break from their studies, and spend two weeks in France to recharge their batteries.

One of Daniels other loves was an old VW camper van which he had cleaned up and was quite respectable, well, respectable for students anyway. "No laptops or mobile phones" he said. "Just us, and see where it takes us". Lizzie was apprehensive about being completely cut off, but liked the idea of taking off for two weeks with no laptops or medical books. So, on Sunday 13th February, they set off for France.

Chapter 4

Born in 1965, Marcus was the son of a pharmacist in Wiesbaden, Germany. He was typically German, fair skinned, blonde hair and blue eyes. He was 6' 2", handsome, and had a dimple in his chin. His father Georg had worked in a pharmacy shop since leaving school, and when the elderly owner retired, he took over, refurbishing the shop to bring it up to date. From an early age, Marcus was very interested in the various products in the pharmacy. He loved helping his father prepare the prescriptions for the customers, and by the age of 10 he knew all of the names and properties of the various drugs held in the store. Even then he knew where his destiny lay. His love of chemistry meant he regularly topped the class at school, in chemistry and biology, and it came as no surprise when he left for the prestigious University of Gottingen, to study chemistry at the ridiculously precocious age of 16. Having achieved a Master's degree by the age of 20, he then took his PhD which he completed at 23. Although he studied hard, he was extremely popular at the University, excelling in winter sports and spent several weekends skiing in the mountains, regularly entertaining a new girlfriend.

Marcus was headhunted by Merck in America, and in October 1989 flew off to New Jersey to begin his working life as a research assistant. He quickly settled in to his new role, with many emails back to his father about the developments he was working on, without giving away any trade secrets of course. He was soon promoted to senior research assistant, and then to research scientist with two assistants of his own. Things were definitely looking up, although his love life had taken a back seat due to long days and evenings in the research lab.

It was in 1991 that he attended a $1000 a plate gala dinner in Manhattan which was subject of an auction, raising funds for the presidential campaign of Ross Perot. Perot was running as an independent, taking on the incumbent, George H.W. Bush, and the upcoming governor of Arkansas, Bill Clinton. Despite withdrawing from the race, then re-joining in October, Perot polled 19% of the popular vote, the highest percentage for an independent since Teddy Roosevelt in 1912.

Aside from his love of chemistry, Marcus was particularly keen on politics, hoping at some stage to progress from research, and felt it necessary to make himself known in the right circles and managed to arrange an introduction to the event. His intention had been purely to make some potentially useful contacts but he had his heart stolen by Stephanie, one of the models wearing a fabulous diamond and emerald necklace.

Stephanie was accustomed to the attention showered on her by handsome young, and not so handsome, not so young men, but she was unsettled by that constant staring of the handsome blonde young man, but somehow, she sensed something...... what was it?...... was it chemistry?....... was it attraction?...... whatever it was she felt it. She felt herself blushing, hoping that everyone would put it down to the very warm evening. Marcus watched her every move as she wound her way around the floor, giving potential bidders the chance to view the necklace but there was no way he could afford the estimated $50,000 to bid for the necklace she was wearing. He found he could not take his eyes off her, and whenever she glanced across at him, he was sure she blushed. He carefully made his way through the crowded room towards the model, and came up behind her. He saw that she was looking around the room for something or someone, then when she turned around, he found himself standing before her. He saw her blush again and then he stumbled over his words, and it was as if he was afraid, afraid she wouldn't like him. He was almost tongue tied but managed to say, "What a lovely necklace, it's a pity it pales into insignificance against the beautiful background". She blushed again, smiled quite prettily, and accepted his offer for dinner later in the week. She found herself looking forward to the evening more than she had expected. He took her to an exclusive Manhattan restaurant where they found they could talk and talk and talk.

Although her parents were American, Stephanie was born and raised in Germany until she was fourteen and spoke German fluently. Her father, Rutherford Wallace Buchanan-Hunt III, had then moved the family back to America, when he transferred from running his company's Frankfurt office, to take over as CEO at the Bank's Head Office in New York. She was tall and willowy, with long blonde hair, which she often wore in a French pleat. She had a pale creamy complexion setting off her hazel eyes which sparkled when she laughed. She had lived in the family's mansion in upstate New York, and spent summers in the Hamptons. Stephanie had had her own pony since she was four, and was an accomplished rider, riding her horse every day and playing tennis most afternoons. She had inherited her good looks from her mother, Georgina, still a strikingly handsome woman, who was heavily involved in charity work, entertained on a lavish scale, and also rode her horse most mornings, before meeting her friends for lunch.

Stephanie was educated at the Birklehof boarding school in the Black Forest, and then the prestigious Emma Willard school in Troy, New York. Not particularly gifted academically, at 17 she was sent to the Swiss finishing school Chateau Mont-Choisi, returning to the States after a year, a poised and self-confident young woman. Stephanie was used to the finer things life had to offer, and could comfortably be described as "high maintenance".

Their house was magnificent. Set in ten acres, with swimming pool, tennis court, four car garage, and stables for six horses. Her father was rich, very very rich, but she only saw him rarely as he spent the week in his Manhattan flat, commuting from their home to the city being so impractical. Her father was also keen to be involved in politics, having aspirations one day to run for office, and in the late 1980's had met Ross Perot who was running for President in 1992. Stephanie was introduced to Perot one evening at a dinner party, and he asked if she would model jewellery at a fund raiser for his presidential campaign. She thought that it would be fun, so agreed. Obviously, she needed a new outfit for the evening. She chose an Oscar de la Renta eau-de-nil full-length gown with a plunging V neck and criss-cross straps at the back, showing off her fabulous tan, trim figure, perfectly matching the diamond and emerald necklace, and setting her father's bank balance back by the GDP of a small American town.

She was radiant as she walked around the room, displaying the fabulous necklace. She became aware of one particular young man with blonde hair, blue eyes and a cute smile, with a dimple in his chin. No, she wasn't paying attention. Everywhere she looked he appeared to be there in her eyeline. She felt herself blushing. He was very attractive. No, she really wasn't paying any attention. She wandered away from him, then looked round for him, but he was gone, her heart sank as she looked around the room but still couldn't see him, she turned around and he was standing right in front of her. He opened his mouth as if to say something, and eventually stammered "What a lovely necklace. Such a pity it pales into insignificance on such a beautiful background ". She blushed again. He was encouraged by her smile and said "Perhaps you would like to have dinner with me one evening," and that was it. She fell in love with him there and then.

Marcus was not a party animal and rarely went out socially, not having a wide circle of friends, concentrating mainly on his career, however he had found out who her family was and splashed out on a Ralph Lauren tailored wool suit with an open neck blue shirt. He picked her up at her father's Manhattan flat at 7 p.m. on their first date and took her to Eleven Madison Park, a restaurant in the flat iron district of New York. Stephanie was wearing a Gianni Versace outfit of white evening trousers with a matching top and white Jimmy Choo high heels. Heads turned as they entered the restaurant and Marcus, dazzled by her beauty was so proud that she was on his arm. The meal was perfect and they found they could talk on many subjects and laughed a lot. Dropping her back at her father's flat Stephanie kissed him goodnight and he drove away with his head in the clouds. A whirlwind courtship followed, a short engagement and a huge wedding, setting back her father's bank balance by the GDP of a small American City.

They moved into a large house in Kenilworth, New Jersey, near to Merck's head office, a wedding gift from her parents, setting her father's bank balance back by the GDP of a small American State. Although large, it was dwarfed by her parent's property. It did have stabling however, so Stephanie was able to bring her horse. Marcus was not a rider although he had promised to take lessons from Stephanie. There was also a tennis court, something they both enjoyed and Marcus was quite an athlete with great hand/eye co-ordination. Although there was no swimming pool, plans were put in place for its construction, a wedding gift from Marcus.

Like most newlyweds, their early years were idyllic. His rise through the ranks at Merck can only be described as meteoric, eventually heading up his own research department. Marcus did spend long hours at work, but he was climbing the corporate ladder very quickly, and they jointly felt that this would prove very advantageous in his later career. Stephanie soon had a large group of friends that met quite regularly for lunch. She found that she was a good cook and was keen to learn new recipes, delighting her new friends at her regular dinner parties. She and Marcus enjoyed a good social life, attending barbecues, parties, dances and the theatre. She loved opera and the ballet, but Marcus was not enamoured, favouring the more popular musicals, Miss Saigon, Guys and Dolls, Phantom of the Opera with the brilliant Michael Crawford, and his favourite, Les Misérables. She joined committees and immersed herself in charity work. She was fast becoming a pillar of society. It was then in 1996 Marcus dropped his bombshell. He thought it was time to leave Merck, branch out and start his own company researching pharmaceuticals, and felt it necessary to relocate to Switzerland. She was devastated he wanted to go to Switzerland and argued vehemently against it, in fact their first real row. She argued, pleaded, and wept, but Marcus would not be moved, so she had to make a decision. Move to Switzerland or leave Marcus. They moved to Switzerland.

Chapter 5

Daniel and Lizzie spent all of Saturday and Sunday cleaning out, then loading up a now spick and span camper van, (Mostly down to Lizzie) and set off on the long drive south to the Eurotunnel terminal at Ashford. It was around 300 miles, and Daniel estimated it would take about six hours of driving. They had booked an early crossing before 6:00 a.m., one of the cheaper crossings to help with the cost of their holiday, so allowing for a break at a motorway service area, and any unforeseen holdups, they left at 10 o'clock on Sunday night. They shared the driving, both dozed a little, and stopped for coffee and pizza around 2 a.m. at a motorway service station. Arriving at the Eurotunnel terminal just before 5, they managed a quick wash to freshen up, then it was time to load the van onto the train and begin their journey into France.

Daniel had spent a holiday with his parents in Annecy many years ago, and remembered walking and cycling in the mountains, so he decided to go there first, and see if his memory hadn't played tricks. He had sold the idea to Lizzie and was a little concerned that it wasn't all rose-coloured specs he was looking through. Lizzie had never been to France, so this was a new experience for her. The only time she had been out of England, was a fortnight in Ibiza with a group of girls from school to celebrate their 'A' level results. It had been great fun, rarely getting to bed before the sun rose, and sleeping until lunch time, then sleeping on the beach, until it was time to get ready to go clubbing again. Annecy was another long drive, at least 8 hours, but they didn't have to do it all in one day. They could take their time and enjoy the French scenery and, being self-contained, stop overnight in one of the many Aire's en-route.

Daniel decided to drive through the centre of Paris, and at least see the sights and show Lizzie the magnificence of the city. Having been stuck in several traffic jams, he decided perhaps it had been a mistake, however they had driven down the Champs-Elysée, where, managing to find a parking spot just as someone was leaving, they had lunch at a small bistro. It was then that Daniel produced a small gift for Lizzie saying "Happy Valentine's Day sweetheart. Je t'aime," "You'll never be able to top this Daniel, but aren't Valentines supposed to be anonymous," she exclaimed opening the box and finding a delicate gold chain with a gold heart shaped locket inside. She opened the locket and saw a photo of her and Daniel on each side. She threw her arms around him and they kissed, much to the delight and applause of the Parisians at the nearby tables. Paris is not known as La Ville de l'Amour (The City of Love) for nothing.

Leaving the bistro hand in hand, with Lizzie wearing her new locket, they circled the Arc-de-Triomphe, managed to see the Tuileries, the Pompidou Centre and finally passed the Eiffel Tower. "Just like Blackpool without the beach" Lizzie said. They had taken photographs of all of the sights, as they had remembered to bring their cameras, but agreed that they would return one day, and spend more time in the wonderful city. After the evening rush hour, they left Paris and stopped at a small roadside restaurant on the main street of a sweet little village, and enjoyed their first French dinner of steak and frites and a bottle of vin de table, for just a few euros. They enjoyed the relaxed atmosphere of the small restaurant and after dinner drove out of the village on the A6, where they pulled into an Aire for the night. They were exhausted after such a long day and the previous all-night drive, and quickly fell into a sound sleep.

The next morning, they were woken by the rumbling of a large articulated lorry pulling into the Aire beside them. It was half past eight, and they were surprised at how refreshed they felt. They had bought croissants from a boulangerie yesterday, so fortified with coffee and the croissants, they set off again. Their route to Annecy was along the less frequented country roads, which did take a little longer, but took them through several quaint sleepy villages, and avoided the tolls on the motorways.

Reaching Annecy in the late afternoon, they drove on into the mountains to find a place to stop for the night, and were able to pull off the road into a small clearing. They had stopped at a Carrefour supermarket to stock up on foodstuffs, and had marvelled at the extensive range of fresh pre-prepared meals at very reasonable prices. Lizzie was used to cooking, having helped at home when her mother was working the late shift at the supermarket, so set to, to make the evening meal, while Daniel rearranged the seating and set the small table. They had bought stuffed mushrooms, coq au vin, and tarte aux pomme, and a very cheap vin rouge to wash it down. After dinner, they stretched their legs walking along the side of the road, which did not seem to be particularly busy, with only a few cars passing them.

The next day they drove back to Annecy, parked the van and walked into the old town which was still as beautiful as he remembered, sitting at the head of the large lake overlooked by wonderful mountain scenery. The old town was quaint, with cafes lining the canals and populated with lots of shoppers and hikers enjoying a coffee or hot chocolate. It was possible to ride along the lake shore on bicycles so they hired two from one of the many cycles and camping shops in the town. Returning to the old town after their ride they then enjoyed a boat ride on the lake. Daniel was particularly interested in seeing the castle, and Lizzie the museum, so they returned to Annecy the following day and visited Chateau d'Annecy, and were impressed by the 12th century Tour de la Reine with its 4-metre-thick walls. A castle was a major part of his computer game, so he enjoyed looking at the structure and layout of the rooms and passages, thinking how he could incorporate this into his game. He took several pictures to remind him so that he could reproduce the atmosphere of the dungeons. Lizzie liked browsing the Museum of Alpine Popular Art and the display of vernacular furniture from the 15th century. Following the visit to the castle and museum, they sat at a café drinking hot chocolate and watching the world go by.

Having seen what Annecy had to offer, they drove out towards Thones, and into the mountains to do some walking. Climbing steeply out of Annecy, they started to run into snow covered trees and roads, and pulled off onto a narrow track to see where it led. Following the track, they started to go down into a valley, and after about 400 yards found a nice little sheltered clearing where they could park. Getting out of the camper van they looked south west over a deep ravine and breathed in the fresh mountain air which was cool and crisp. Some of the trees, still with snow covered branches, were showing signs of returning to life after their winter break, and the birds were chirping whilst building their nests. The spot they had found was peaceful and idyllic. The next two days were spent exploring the area, hiking along well-worn footpaths, climbing to the top of the Col des Avaris observation deck and enjoying the breath-taking views, and taking photographs to share with those back home. Sitting on the observation deck, Lizzie asked Daniel if they could go to Chamonix or Geneva. "Certainly," replied Daniel, "which would you prefer," "Well, both would be nice, but Chamonix sounds more fashionable, and skiing is something I might like to try some time, not now, but someday perhaps. It would be nice to see the town. It has such a famous name; I would like to go there. Might even do a little shopping," she said smiling. "First thing tomorrow then, its only about 90 minutes away so we could easily get there and back in a day, then in a couple of days we will go to Geneva."

Next morning, an early alarm and breakfast, then back into the centre of Thones and on to the D909. It was another bright sunny morning and again they marvelled at the wonderful scenery as they crossed the snow-capped mountainous route into Chamonix. The town sits at the base of Mont Blanc on the border between Italy and Switzerland, has well signposted walks and is full of fashionable shops and restaurants. Daniel and Lizzie strolled through the town and sat at an outside table for a hot chocolate each. "Would you like to go up a ski lift?" asked Daniel, "Yes, that would be lovely," So, they followed signs to the ski lifts and found that Le Brevent had only a short queue. They bought their return tickets for the lift and felt a little underdressed as they were the only ones without ski clothes and equipment. They thoroughly enjoyed the ride in the lift up to Planpraz, and then joined the queue for the next cable car up to the summit at Le Brevent. They dismounted the cable car and watched the skiers putting on their skis and then setting off back down the mountain. All of the skiers seemed to be expert and showed off their skills slaloming down the mountainside.

They booked a late lunch at Restaurant La Panoramic, and sat outside at a table enjoying a lunch of French onion soup, medium rare steak with frites and a tarte au tatin. "I'm going to be enormous when I get back home," Lizzie said, "You're not the only one," Daniel replied. They took the return cable cars back to Chamonix and spent a couple of hours browsing the designer shops, although at the prices being charged, they were only window shopping. They found a bar where they listened to the live music and had a couple of beers before heading back to Thones and parking again on their track.

The clouds looked ominous next morning, and Daniel suggested that they go out for a short walk before it snowed, so just after breakfast they wrapped up in warm and waterproof clothes, filled a flask with coffee, took a couple of pastries, walked up the track towards the road and set off along a well-worn footpath through the trees. It started to snow. Fine flakes at first, but soon followed by larger ones. They stopped for their coffee and pastries around mid-morning and then the snow started to intensify, so they hurried back to the camper for lunch just as the snowfall turned into a blizzard. Daniel and Lizzie were getting used to their regular lunch of a long baguette loaf with cheese and patè, a bottle of vin blanc, and decided to sit tight in the warm camper during the snowstorm.

They got out some of the games they had brought with them, Scrabble, Monopoly, Cluedo, Yahtzee and the old favourite Trivial Pursuit, opened another bottle of wine and decided on Monopoly. The game can, and did, go on for some time and it wasn't until after Lizzie had finally bankrupted Daniel, when, realising it had turning dark, they looked out of the camper and saw that the snow had stopped but the landscape had completely changed into a winter wonderland with everything covered in a thick blanket of snow. They stepped outside but found they were almost knee deep in the snow, "It looks wonderful, but I have a feeling we are going to be stuck for a while," said Daniel. "We did stock up at the supermarket, so we should be OK for several days," replied Lizzie.

"Let's hope so, we may as well have an early night and see what tomorrow brings," They went to bed and slept soundly, although the vin blanc may have helped.

Chapter 6

The day started quietly enough for Izzy. Klara had been an angel, waking up smiling, allowing herself to be dressed and eating her breakfast without the usual drama. Izzy was getting used to the histrionics, and had put this down to the change in nanny in the last couple of months, but was hopeful that this was about to change. She had played lots of games with Klara and was trying to win her trust and confidence, without spoiling her.

Marcus had rented a chalet in Chamonix for a week, and while he and Stephanie honed their skills on the pistes, Klara had enjoyed tobogganing with Izzy, and then Izzy, no mean skier herself, had tried putting her on skis and letting her slide down a small slope. Children need to be about 4 or 5 before learning to ski properly, but this had just been a little bit of fun. Klara had done very well, only falling over a couple of times, but she was obviously enjoying it. No doubt when she was older, she would progress as a skier, given the passion Marcus and Stephanie had for the sport. They had built a snowman together and had had little snowball fights with Alex and at one stage Alex had grabbed Izzy and rubbed fresh snow into her face in a playful way. She could still remember the tingle she had felt, and had stopped struggling against him, turning and looking straight into his eyes and smiled. Alex had smiled back and Izzy was sure he was going to kiss her, but after a few seconds, which seemed like hours, he just released her from his grip and turned away and went over to where Klara was playing in the snow.

Gerry had not slept well last night. The excitement of driving the new van, and Liverpool's televised match had kept him awake since

3 a.m. He rose at 4, showered, dressed in his UPS uniform, and was at the warehouse before 5, to take out his new pride and joy. Liverpool's anthem was running through his brain.
"When you walk through a storm, keep your head up high, and don't be afraid of the dark".

Izzy remembered having an enjoyable family holiday in Annecy when she had been 10 or 11, and as Marcus and Stephanie were skiing again today, had asked Alex to drive them to Annecy to see the lake and the old town. Izzy was really looking forward to today's outing with Alex, oh, and not forgetting they would be taking Klara of course. Annecy was well named the Venice of the Alps, with the Canal-du-Vassé and the very short River Thiou running through the centre of the old town, and many smaller canals linking in to them. Fed from Lake Annecy the Canal-du-Vassé joins the River Thiou and then the Fier, which is a tributary of the Rhone. When Alex had collected her from the airport in Geneva, six weeks ago, Izzy's heart had skipped a beat, and she looked forward to every minute spent with him. She had flirted with him outrageously, demure one minute, provocative the next, and was sure he was responding to her charms.

The warehousemen had loaded up the van and Gerry was given the delivery sheet. He also had to make three pick-ups from collection points and one from a regular industrial site. It had snowed heavily through the night, and the forecast for the day was more snow. He was conscious of the tight schedule that meant he would just about be able to see the start of the match, if there were no unforeseen circumstances.

That morning at the ski slopes, Marcus had asked Alex, "Alex, pick us up at 5.15 please," "Yes Mr Meier," Despite several request to do so, Alex could not bring himself to address his employer by his first name, nor could he call Mrs Meier 'Stephanie' as she had implored several times. When he returned from the ski slopes, they packed up the car with all the paraphernalia needed for a nearly three-year-old, and there was quite a bit. After Alex had left with Marcus and Stephanie, she had changed from her quite conservative top and trousers into a rather cleavage revealing blouse and short skirt, not quite a pelmet, but precariously close. Alex returned from the ski slopes and Izzy noticed his eyes opened wide when he saw the outfit she was wearing. She put on a warm fleecy jacket and dressed Klara in warm clothes and boots. Alex stayed with Izzy and Klara all morning, taking a short boat ride on the lake, viewing the mountains from a different perspective. The old town was beautiful, and they strolled the cobbled streets alongside the canals, eating tartiflette and crepes at one of the many cafes overlooking the canal. In the afternoon a boat ride on the lake provided a view of the mountains from a different perspective. They sat together, Klara sometimes between them, sometimes leaning over the rail, Izzy holding her tightly. A very pleasant way to spend the day, and finally treating Klara, and themselves, to ice cream at the famed Les Glacier des Alps. She did not correct the shopkeeper who asked Klara, "and what flavour would mummy like,"

The morning had started off quite well for Gerry, and the first dozen deliveries were made promptly without any hiccups. He had difficulty with the 13th delivery, and it wasn't even a Friday. The address on the package wasn't accurate, and he lost over half-an-hour trying to locate the property. He eventually found the right house, delivered the parcel, and tried to get back onto his tight schedule.
"At the end of the storm there's a golden sky and the sweet silver song of a lark"

Izzy had wanted to look around the castle and museum, Chateau d'Annecy, but Klara was getting restless. Alex kept a watch on Klara, while Izzy bought another top to go with a skirt she had bought in Chamonix. She tried it on and posed for Alex, asking if he approved. It seemed like he did from the look on his face. Alex and Izzy were getting to know each other and Izzy was hopeful that the relationship would develop. She fancied Alex like crazy and was hoping he felt the same, or would do so soon. The weather had been dry and clear in the morning, but snow was forecast for later in the day, Izzy hoping that it would not disrupt their homeward journey and delay the evenings fun.

From the disaster of the 13th drop, the day progressed quite smoothly for Gerry, picking up from two of the collection points, and at a quarter to two he stopped for his lunch, a little later than usual, but driving the van was giving him so much pleasure, time seemed to fly by. Finishing his sandwiches and coffee, he started off again making more deliveries. Soon he would be down to the last three in the town at the bottom of the pass.
"Walk on through the wind, walk on through the rain, though your dreams be tossed and blown".

With Izzy's shopping safely stored in the boot, Alex began their drive home. Klara was securely strapped into the child seat in the rear of the Mercedes limousine, and Izzy sat beside Alex in the front. They made their way through the town just as the first flakes of snow began to fall, putting extra thickness onto the already snow-covered roads. Their route was on main dual carriageway roads, and Izzy was hoping that Alex would get them home safely, and on time, despite the worsening weather. Unfortunately, as they drove down a one-way street, they came across a line of traffic when a car several places ahead of them had skidded across a junction and collided with a large lorry and blocking the road. There was nowhere for them to go, and frustratingly, they were held up for almost an hour. The police and ambulances soon arrived, and then the fire service had to cut the driver out of the car before they managed to clear the traffic jam.

The snow was getting heavier and was now a thick covering on the roads. Gerry had been able to make his last pick-ups from the third collection point and the industrial site and he had to drive up into the mountains, get over the pass, and make it to the next town for his final three deliveries.

Eventually they were allowed to proceed, and managed to get out of the town without further mishap. Joining the dual carriageway, a roadside information sign warned of a further delay because of another accident. Alex said he knew a short cut, so left the dual carriageway at the next junction. The roads were not as easy to drive on, but the distance was a little shorter than the main road, so he decided to try to make up time over the mountain pass. Alex kept looking at his watch, it was now 4.48, and it was touch-and-go if he would be able to get back home in time to collect Marcus and Stephanie and drive them to a party later that evening, so he pulled over into a layby and sent a text to Marcus. "Sorry Mr Meier, we have been held up by an accident in the centre of Annecy for almost an hour. I don't think I can get to you much before 6.15. Can you get back to the chalet under your own steam," "Don't worry Alex," Marcus replied, "we can get a taxi. See you there, are you all OK?" "Yes, we are all fine, just frustrated, couldn't go anywhere. I'm making a detour now. Klara's asleep in her seat."

Driving in these conditions was proving more difficult for Gerry, and Mr Johannsson's words were ringing in his ears, "Don't scratch it", but he was keen to get home to see the match. He picked up his speed.

Izzy's mouth had run dry, her hand on his right thigh. Alex was getting aroused; she could feel that. She smiled inwardly to herself. It was going to be a good night.

Gerry was running out of time. The van was handling beautifully and he was gaining confidence from its road holding but the snow was heavier now and he was pushing the van as fast as he dared. It would take time to get back to the depot, complete his paperwork, then back to the flat to watch the game.

Alex concentrated on his driving, Izzy sitting beside him staring through the windscreen at the falling snow, her hand resting nonchalantly on his right thigh.

The pass over the mountains was narrow in places with lots of bends, meaning Gerry was constantly changing gear to keep control. The snow was reflecting in his headlight beams making it difficult to see clearly. The rocks on the side of the mountain kept looming out of the snow and he was conscious of his responsibility for the van. *"Walk on, walk on, with hope in your heart, and you'll never walk alone"*

Alex smiled inwardly to himself. Izzy was sitting beside him at the moment, looking straight ahead, her left hand on his right thigh. He felt himself getting aroused. It was going to be a good night after all. He started to speed up.

Rounding one bend, the van nearly skidded into the rocks, but Gerry managed to regain control. Pushing on, he took a right hand bend a little too quickly, and slid sideways across the road towards the barriers. As he did so, he saw headlights coming towards him. "Don't scratch it", ringing in his ears. His heart was in his mouth as he braked and turned the steering wheel to the left to counteract the skid. The van started to straighten up.

Izzy looked across at Alex and saw the slight smile cross his lips, but then his face changed, his body stiffened, and it had nothing to do with her left hand. "Christ Almighty" he yelled. She looked at the road and saw a large van snaking towards them. All she could see was a large UPS sign on the side of the van. Surely it was impossible to miss it.

Gerry grimaced, braked hard, and pulled his steering wheel hard left. The back end of the van tucked in behind him. A dark limo shot past him on the left-hand side, and disappeared around the corner.

A strangled scream gurgled in Izzy's throat. Alex wrenched the wheel to the right, as the van straightened up and they missed each other by millimetres.

Gerry was shaking and in a cold sweat. He looked in his mirrors but could see nothing. "Shit, that was close," he said to himself, breathing a huge sigh of relief, and slowed down almost to a crawl.

Alex had lost control of the car on the snow-covered road, and the Limo slid into the side barriers with an almighty bang. A couple of the side air bags deployed and Alex couldn't see where he was going. This sent them skidding back across the road and into the rocks on the side of the mountain, again a sickening crash. Izzy screamed, Klara woke up and started crying. Alex was fighting to regain control, but the car overturned and bounced back across the road, hurtling over the edge barriers, and down into the ravine.

Suddenly they were flying, falling, and crashing into the rocks on the side of the ravine. Glass showered over them as the windows smashed. The remaining airbags came at the from all angles. Klara cried out, Izzy screamed and screamed, seeing trees coming to meet them as they gathered momentum and a huge branch smashed through the windscreen impaling the car and Alex, and bringing it to sudden stop. The car was upside down. Izzy groaned "Alex" There was no reply. "Alex," Again, no reply. Izzy felt her eyes closing. She could hear Klara crying faintly, the sound fading. "Klara," She whispered. "Kla.....," and her eyes closed forever.

The tree groaned under the impact, and then slowly, under the weight of the car, the branch holding the car bent, creaked, and then snapped, the car crashing to the ground at the base of the tree.

Then nothing.

Silence

Chapter 7

It had snowed all day, and was now quite deep around the camper. Daniel and Lizzie had stayed in the van all day relaxing, playing games and reading books. They had thought about going out into the snowstorm, but decided against it. Their clothes would have got wet and space for drying them in the van was limited. However, it was getting dark and had stopped snowing and it was a little stuffy in the van, so Daniel and Lizzie took a couple of beers, wrapped themselves up in scarves, hats and gloves against the cold and stood outside to get some fresh air. The sky was clear and full of stars, the air crisp and clear, and they drank their beers, looking into the night sky, marvelling at the constellations, trying to identify them and cuddled together for warmth.

They could see headlights on the road on the other side of the valley, obviously workers coming home after their day at the office or factory. The road wasn't busy but they were fascinated by the lights sweeping round the bends, sometimes lighting the snow-covered mountainside up, sometimes like searchlights into the night sky. It was a mesmerising sight.

Two sets of headlights approached each other, they seemed to pass and one set vanished around a bend, but the other set seemed to pirouette, headlights shining onto the mountain, then into the sky, and then, ... down into the valley. Somersaulting down the mountainside, bouncing on the rocks, down to the bottom of the ravine, and then stopping, its headlights extinguished. They stood shocked and open mouthed as the noise of the crash reached them. The other vehicle had disappeared around the bend and was nowhere in sight. A few seconds passed although it seemed like an eternity. Surely the other vehicle would return. Surely the driver would know he had been involved in an accident. Surely....
All they could hear was silence.
But the other vehicle did not stop.
Did not return.

All thoughts of the match now out of his mind, Gerry had slowed down to a crawl and took some deep breaths. "Phew," he thought, "No damage done." He stopped shaking. He slowly picked up speed and two kilometres further on, there was a lay-by, a photo opportunity popular with tourists during the summer to take pictures of the mountains and valley. He pulled in and drank the remaining dregs of coffee from his flask. He got out of the van, took some deep breaths of the fresh mountain air and on shaky legs walked around the van to check for damage using his torch. Nothing. He realised that he had been holding his breath and breathed again. He walked up and down the layby trying to calm down and pull himself together. His legs felt a little stronger so he got back into the van and slowly pulled back out onto the road. Perhaps I can see the second half he thought to himself
"You'll never walk alone"

What was that! "Lizzie, did you hear something?" "Yes, I think so. Was that a cry?" Daniel and Lizzie stood there in the silence. Again, they heard something, what was that? Was it a cry? was it an animal? they strained to listen. No there it was again. Yes, yes it was a cry. There was someone alive in the car.

Marcus was fuming, his face like thunder. "Where are they? why haven't they called?" "I'm sure there is a reasonable explanation" Stephanie said, trying to calm him, but she was worried too. "Maybe the batteries are flat on their cells," Being American, Stephanie hadn't got used to the idea of calling them mobiles. They were now late for the party. They had enjoyed a good days skiing, and had returned to the chalet by taxi after the text from Alex, expecting to see Alex, Izzy and Klara, but the chalet was empty. No sign of the car either. Marcus was renowned for his short temper when things weren't going smoothly at work, but did not usually bring it home with him. He was pacing the chalet like a caged animal. He called Alex again. No reply, straight to voicemail. "Alex where the hell are you. We should be on our way by now, call me," Stephanie called Izzy.
Same result, similar voicemail message left. They had showered and changed for the party, still expecting them to turn up, but that was an hour ago and still no sign. They tried both cell phones again, but although they heard the ringing tone, their calls went through to voicemail every time. "This isn't like Izzy," Stephanie said "There must be something wrong. She always keeps in touch," They both paced the floor, unable to sit down. "I'm calling the police," Marcus finally said. "Get them to check for accidents. Where were they going Steph?" "Annecy wasn't it," Marcus had the list of emergency numbers given to all tourists in the chalet and found the number for the local police. He dialled 17. "What is your emergency?" the voice on the other end asked. "Well, I'm not really sure, but can you tell me if there have been any road accidents between Annecy and Chamonix. My daughter has not been brought home, and my wife

and I are very worried." "Let me check sir," then after a few moments, "yes sir there was an accident between a lorry and a white van on the D909. What kind of vehicle would your daughter be driving sir?" "Oh er she wouldn't have been driving, she's not yet three. Our car is a black Mercedes E55AMG." "Well in that case no sir, no reports of that car being involved in an accident. I can transfer you to the hospital number if you would like." "Yes, please that would be helpful." Marcus was placed on hold with some annoying electronic musak in his ears. Eventually, "Chamonix hospital, how may I help you?" "My name is Marcus Meier, have you had a little girl of almost three, Klara Meier, brought in this afternoon, possibly with a young lady and a man of about 30?" "No sir we have had no admissions this afternoon." "Is there anywhere else I should try?" "Not for an accident sir, this is where they would come." "Thank you for your help." He hung up the phone and to Stephanie said "Nothing at the accident hospital, and apparently nowhere else." "Where can they be?"

The party was forgotten as they anxiously waited for the return of Klara, Izzy and Alex. "Izzy usually calls her mum every evening, I'll get her number and see if she's been in touch," Stephanie found the number. "Hello Mrs Hunter-Smythe, it's Stephanie Meier. I'm sorry to trouble you, but have you heard from Izzy today?" "No, why what's happened?" "We're not sure but she had taken Klara to Annecy with Alex our chauffeur, and they were supposed to have returned about two hours ago but they are not back yet. I know that they were stuck in Annecy following a road closure or something, so I'm sure it's nothing to worry about, but we were just wondering if she'd been in touch," "No, no I haven't heard from her since yesterday evening. She was fine then and saying how much she was enjoying looking after Klara," "I'm sure everything will be fine; I'll tell her to call you," Now of course another family was worried. "Where can they be. Should I drive into Annecy, see if I can see them" Stephanie said. "That's no use now" said Marcus,

"It's far too late, and too dark to see anything. The police might be out looking, and we are better off staying here in case they return," "But I must do something. Where can they be?" "Where are they?"

Chapter 8

"Surely, that driver will come back. Surely."
"Surely, he'll come back. Surely".
Daniel and Lizzie kept repeating that over and over for several minutes. "The police will be here in a minute," They could still hear the cry. But no police. No blue lights. No sirens. No one stopped. There were still the odd headlights from cars traveling along the narrow road, rounding the bend, lighting up the mountainside and then out into the darkening night sky like searchlights, but no blue lights. No sirens. No one stopped. They could still hear a cry. Then they said, almost in unison. "We'll have to go down there, see if we can help."

They went back into the camper, and Lizzie made a flask of hot coffee to take with them. They dressed in their warmest clothes, gloves and woolly hats and set off down the side of the valley towards the crash site. They had torches, but little else. Nothing in the way of tools. Lizzie did think to bring the first aid kit out of the camper. It was small, but at least it had dressings and antiseptic. It might be of some use. It was slow going and it had started to snow again. Then Daniel said "I'd better go back and put the hazard lights on, otherwise we might not be able to find our way back," So, turning around, he retraced his steps back to the camper and switched on the hazard lights. Returning to Lizzie he said "It is a good job I went back; our footprints are almost covered in this snow. I did not put the heater on as we are not there. I didn't want the camper to go up in flames,"

41

They clambered down over rocks, slipping and sliding down the side of the valley, bumping into trees that appeared out of the snow. The snow was deep, well up to their knees and more than once they fell headlong into the snow. But still, they could hear the cry. It was getting louder, so they felt they were getting closer. They could not see more than 5 metres through the blizzard, and were now completely soaked and cold. After what seemed like a lifetime, but was probably only about 45 minutes, they seemed to be climbing again so must have reached the bottom. They thought the car had come almost down to the floor of the valley, and hoped they could find it soon. The cry was now quite loud and they were sure it was a child wailing.

They struggled on further, then Lizzie said, "Just a minute Daniel I think the cry is getting further away. We must have missed it," They stopped, listened and sure enough the cry seemed further away now. They retraced their steps, taking a slightly higher route up the mountainside. Then they saw it, at the base of a large tree. A mangled wreck, impaled on a tree branch, upside down on its roof. They clambered up over some rocks and saw the smashed windows and heard the child's cry. The driver's door was wedged tight, but the window was smashed. Lizzie lay down on the snow-covered ground looking through the driver's window. The driver was slumped against the steering wheel, the tree branch through the windscreen either against, or into, his chest. "Hello," Lizzie called. No answer. "Hello there, can you hear me? are you alright?" She called again. Lizzie reached in and felt for a pulse. Nothing. "Oh Daniel, I'm sure the drivers dead." She looked across, shining her torch on the passenger. A pretty young girl was staring lifelessly into space. "Do you think you could check the passenger; she doesn't look good." Daniel scrambled round to the other side of the car and leaned in through the shattered passenger door window. "Hi there, can you hear me? are you OK?" No answer. He checked the pulse on the young girl's neck. "Lizzie, I think she's dead too." A small child was hanging upside down in a car seat in the rear, sobbing.

Lizzie went to the rear of the car. Snow had blown in through the broken windows covering the roof, and there was a light covering on the child, a girl of about 2 or 3, "What have we here. There, There. Don't worry, I'll look after you. Are you going to be my brave little girl"? Lizzie managed to pull the rear door open, leaned in and brushed the snow off the child and carefully checked her for any obvious signs of injury, but she appeared to be unhurt. Unbuckling the child seat straps, Lizzie gathered the girl into her arms, soothing her. The wailing continued. Although both Daniel and Lizzie had been to funerals of grandparents, neither of them had actually ever seen a dead person before, Lizzie's course not yet having got round to dealing with dead bodies, so they were both in a state of shock. They tried to give the child some of the hot tea from the flask but she wouldn't drink it. "We must get this little one back to the van and some warmth," said Lizzie. "She's freezing, I don't want her to get hypothermia."

So, they headed back, hoping to follow their tracks before the snow completely covered them. If not, it could be difficult to find the van in these conditions. It had taken them over an hour to get to the car, and it would take longer to get back as most of the time it would be uphill, and carrying a child. They shared the load between them, tucking the child inside their own coats, helping each other over the rocks, and pulling themselves up the slopes, often sliding back down until they fell against rocks or trees. In the morning they would both have several cuts and bruises to show for their efforts. Their path down the hillside was still visible, although it probably would not be for much longer if the snow kept falling at this rate. They kept a sharp lookout for the hazard lights on the van, Daniel hoping the battery hadn't gone flat, but there was no sign as yet. It was nearly an hour and a half later before they saw the lights blinking through the snow. They reached the track, opened the van door and, collapsing onto the floor, wept with joy.

Daniel got up from the floor, lit the gas fire and got some dry blankets for the little girl. Lizzie undressed the little girl from her wet clothes and wrapped her in the warm blankets and one of Lizzies jumpers, which covered most of her legs, and put a pair of Lizzies socks on her tiny feet which were blue with the cold. They stripped off their own wet clothes and changed, pulling on warm dry clothes. They were all shivering. Daniel made more hot drinks while Lizzie cuddled the child, whose crying had thankfully stopped. The child had a small cut on the side of her cheek and had a trickle of blood down to her chin which had congealed. It didn't look anything serious and Lizzie was happy that there was no obvious head injury. She cleaned up the cut and found a small plaster in the first aid kit while Daniel heated some soup and they slowly fed the girl, which was quite difficult as she clung tightly to Lizzie. The gas fire was quite efficient and soon had the inside of the van nice and warm, although it was quite steamy with their wet clothes drying. They snuggled up under the blankets on the bed and with the child between them, hugged each other until gradually their bodies warmed up and they felt almost human again. Then tiredness took over and they slept. They were woken a couple of times through the night by the little girl crying, but with soothing words and cuddles, Lizzie soon got her back to sleep.

Marcus and Stephanie were now seriously worried and starting to panic. They hadn't eaten and couldn't sleep. Further calls to the police provided no answers. Izzy's mum called but Stephanie was unable to give her any news. "I'll call as soon as I hear from Izzy," Stephanie promised. They sat down on the sofa, then a few minutes later got up and paced the floor, then sat down again, not quite knowing what to do with themselves. Every few minutes they called the mobiles of Alex and Izzy, but the voicemail was all they heard. They eventually fell into an exhausted troubled sleep on the sofa.

Chapter 9

Daniel and Lizzie woke to a bright sunny morning. It had snowed for most of the night and the landscape was pristine. Looking down the valley, they could see no sign of their footprints or the car. The track back up to the road was deep with snow and impassable. Fortunately, they had stocked up the larder and had plenty of water. The little girl was very quiet and looked suspiciously at both Daniel and Lizzie, but she did drink a glass of milk and ate a small bowl of porridge, before starting to cry again. Lizzie cuddled her in her arms, and slowly the crying stopped, the child snuggling up against her. "There, There. Don't worry, little one, I'll look after you. Are you going to be my brave little girl"? She promised. "What are we going to do," Lizzie asked. "I've never looked after a little girl, or even baby sat," "We can't get out of here at present. We'll just have to wait until there's a bit of a thaw and we can get moving again," Daniel replied. "I think you're doing fine; I think you'd make a wonderful mother, and she certainly seems to like you. Perhaps we should take her outside and play in the snow, and maybe build a snowman. Try to cheer her up and take her mind off that awful accident," "That's a good idea, she might like that, would you like to build a snowman," Lizzie asked the little girl. All she got in response was a stare. So, they dressed her up in her own clothes which had dried overnight, and then one of Lizzie's sweaters on top, with a woolly hat which swamped her little head. Fortunately, she had been wearing little boots which had also dried. She looked just like the Michelin Man logo and they all went outside into the snow.

It was 8 a.m. and Marcus and Stephanie hadn't slept much. They were drawn and haggard. Stephanie was distraught and could not stop crying. "Where are they Marcus? What can have happened to them?" she kept asking. "I just can't say" he replied "It's quite beyond me. If they had had any problem with the car Alex would have called me. I'll call the police again," But there were still no reports of any accident. Marcus called all of the hospital's in Annecy, Chamonix, and anywhere else close-by he could think of. No one answering their descriptions had been admitted. All the hospitals said much the same thing, that any accident would have been taken to the emergency department at Chamonix hospital. Marcus' mind was starting to play tricks on him, and the lack of sleep was also having an effect. He had an awful feeling. "If they haven't been in an accident, could they have been taken intentionally," Marcus said. "I'd better inform the police they are missing. What if they've all been kidnapped?" Stephanie was horrified, "Kidnapped? Who would take them?" "Well, we do have a reasonable amount of money, we're not what you would call poor. Maybe somebody, I don't know, a criminal gang or something. I don't think it will be Alex or Izzy. Unless that text yesterday was a lie," "Surely it wouldn't be Alex or Izzy. They wouldn't do such a thing. Izzy has been so dependable, Klara adores her, and Alex is a brilliant chauffeur, I'm certain it can't be them taking her away," "I don't really think I mean them, either of them, but this text worries me. Maybe it's not their fault, as I said, maybe they have all been taken by some criminals. Maybe they've been forced to send that text. What else do you think can have happened," "I don't know, I hadn't thought of them all being kidnapped, it is possible I suppose. You don't think it's Alex and Izzy, do you?" "No, I don't, not really, but I'm just trying to make sense of it all," "You don't think it's too soon to call the police, do you?" "I'm not sure, I mean, what else do you suggest, I really don't know what to do. There doesn't appear to be any good reason why they aren't back here, and I just want our little girl back, safe and sound. If they've all been taken, or even if they've taken her, then time is of the essence, and if we do nothing, we may come to regret it," "Very well, you're right of course, it's better than doing nothing."

Marcus rang the police, reported them missing and fifteen minutes later a police officer arrived at the chalet. "Good morning, Monsieur Meier? Did you report missing persons?" "Yes officer, I did. Please come in," "I am Major Guillaume of the Police Municipale," He showed his identity card and was shown into their lounge. "I don't know if we have done the right thing in calling you, we don't want to waste police time. We are not sure what has happened, but our nanny Izzy took our daughter Klara out for the day in the car. They were driven by our chauffeur Alex. They were supposed to return last night and Alex was to pick us up at the ski slopes, then drive my wife and I to a party in Chamonix. He sent us a text to say he could not collect us from the ski slopes on time due to a road closure which had delayed them but that he would meet us here. We got a taxi back here, but when we got back here there was no sign of any of them or the car. We waited and called their mobile phones but everything went through to voicemail," "You were quite right to call us sir, and that is not wasting our time. We need to act on this at once. We take missing children as a top priority, and if she has been taken away it is kidnapping, which is a very serious crime.

With your permission we will monitor your phones in case of any ransom demands, put out a call to Interpol, the airport's and border controls. Of course, in the EU they could drive anywhere, and by now could be at least eight or nine hundred miles away. We will obviously check the road closure in Annecy. Can you provide me with any photographs of the missing persons?" "Yes of course." Stephanie had lots of pictures of Klara on her mobile phone and was able to pick the best one and send it to the policeman. She was also able to find a good one of Izzy with Klara and sent that as well. Marcus had a photo of Alex which he forwarded. "Thank you. I shall immediately send these photos and my report to Capitaine Cadieux, who is in charge of such matters, and I will now go back to the station to begin circulating the details,"

Chapter 10

Within half an hour Capitaine Cadieux was at their door and introduced himself, showing his police identification. Antoine Cadieux was a short tubby man with a round cherubic face, rosy cheeks, short dark hair with a centre parting and a neatly trimmed moustache and goatee beard which did not suit him. Behind rimless glasses, his eyes were a steely grey which appeared to dart everywhere taking in his surroundings at first glance. His voice was soft and gentle and he had a caring manner. He was shown into the lounge and sat opposite Stephanie and Marcus, who said "Thank you for coming Capitaine. We're not quite sure what has happened, all we know is that Klara, our daughter, is missing, along with Alex, the chauffeur and Izzy, the nanny. The first police officer, Major Guillaume I think he said his name was, seemed to imply kidnapping was a possibility but as far as we know, both Alex and Izzy are happy here. They are well paid and seem to enjoy their work. We don't think that they would have taken Klara away."

Capitaine Cadieux gently began his questioning. "I have read the report from Major Guillaume, but will assume nothing and I assure you that my team and I will leave no stone unturned to find your daughter, the driver, and nanny, whatever the circumstances. I appreciate that both of you are distressed and concerned at present, but it is most important that I find out as much as I can so that I can instruct my team on their enquiries. I will try not to upset you further, but my questions are vital in trying to locate your daughter, and I apologise if any questions seem repetitive or cause offence, but I do need to ask some difficult questions." "Yes of course Capitaine" replied Marcus "We will answer any questions you have," Marcus and Stephanie sat side by side holding hands, Stephanie, holding a large box of tissues, wiping away tears which would not stop falling.

He began with Marcus. "Monsieur Meier Is there anything from your business dealings that could have an influence on this," "No, nothing," "You carry out research into pharmaceuticals, is that right?" "Yes, I have my own company, and we are heavily involved in trying to produce new drugs." "Is this a lucrative business?" "Well... erm... yes I suppose it is." "How many staff do you employ." "15" "Is that including yourself?" "No, I am in addition to that." "Are you aware of anyone who might have a grudge against you" "No" "Do you have competitors that might be wanting to harm your business?" "No, I get on well with all of my colleagues in the research field," "Are you tendering for any contracts at present?" "No, we are far too busy to be looking for more work," "Has anyone left the company recently for any reason?" "Again, no. No-one has left the company for over two years; I think we have a very contented workforce." "Have you received any threats of any kind?" "No, not at all," "Have you noticed anyone hanging around outside the chalet, at home or your office?" "No, I can't say I've noticed anything or anyone unusual," "The three missing persons, when did you last see each of them," "It was yesterday morning about 7.30 when I kissed Klara goodbye, she had not yet had her breakfast and Izzy was with her getting her dressed. Alex was driving us to the ski slopes so he left us there around 8.25 a.m. and was supposed to collect us about 5.15. I think Izzy had arranged for them all to go out for the day somewhere, although I don't actually remember where they said," "They were going to go to Annecy," Stephanie reminded him. Marcus looked over at Stephanie and smiled his thanks. "And did he not pick you up," "No, he sent a text saying they were held up due to an accident and could not get back before 6.15 and could I get back under my own steam. I said yes of course. We took a taxi," "Do you still have that text?" "Yes, here it is," Marcus handed over his phone to Cadieux who read the text, noted that it had been sent at 4.48 and returned it to Marcus. "Could you forward that text to me please, to this number," and gave Marcus his mobile number. Marcus forwarded the text. "And you haven't heard from him since," "No nothing at all. Everything goes straight to voicemail," "Mm..," Cadieux stroked his chin. "Does the car have a tracker fitted." "It does, but it had developed a fault and the car is booked in for repair when we return from holiday," "How long ago was the fault noticed," "I am not sure exactly; it was Alex who came to me about ten days ago and said he had checked it and it wasn't working and should he book the repair, I said yes of course," "Does Alex carry out the servicing and maintenance to the car?" "No, the servicing is carried out at the main dealer in Lausanne, but day to day things, like oil, tyres and fuel, he takes care of," "Do you drive the car Monsieur Meier?" "Marcus please Capitaine, yes I do drive occasionally, but mostly Alex takes care of the driving. In the morning going to work I am checking my emails on my phone and after work I am usually too tired to concentrate on the roads." "You did not notice the tracker not working," "No, I don't think I have driven for about a month. I have been heavily involved in a new research project, working long hours so Alex takes me to work and brings me home at night, usually very tired and often quite late," "Very late," said Stephanie pointedly. "Mm.... Thank you Marcus" mused Cadieux looking at Stephanie and stroking his chin again.

He then turned to Stephanie. "Madame Meier, if I may," "Capitaine you must call me Stephanie please," Cadieux smiled his thanks "Thank you Stephanie, have you been aware of anyone hanging around your home in Lausanne or here at the chalet?" "Sorry no." "Have you received any strange telephone calls, perhaps no-one on the line when you answer?" "Sorry no." "Does Klara attend a kindergarten or anything similar?" "Yes, two mornings a week she goes to a kindergarten playschool." "Who takes her?" "Usually, the nanny and at present that is Izzy, and Alex drives them." "Why do you say at present that is Izzy?" "Well, she has only been with us since the beginning of January" "Any problems with the parents of other children?" "Sorry no." "There's no need to apologise Stephanie," again Cadieux smiled at Stephanie, "there is no right or wrong answer, only truthful ones. Have you had any problems with Izzy over Klara," "No, quite the opposite in fact. Izzy loves Klara, and Klara seems to love her." "And do you drive the car, Stephanie?" "No, well yes now and then, but I haven't actually driven the car since before Christmas," "You did seem a little upset at the hours your husband is working at present," "Honestly, yes, it is a little concerning, sometimes we are a little like ships that pass in the night, but Marcus has said that this is a difficult research project, at a tricky point and it needs his full-time supervision to get it right. He doesn't work late all the time, and hasn't done so often, it's just at present that seems to be the case. We do try to have at least one full day together as a family every week, and it was Marcus who suggested that we have this little holiday together," "Forgive me for asking, but is your marriage happy?" "Yes, I believe so. I would think at least as happy as most married couples. We have been married for 12 years with a beautiful daughter and I still love Marcus deeply," "And I her," interjected Marcus, "what are you implying Capitaine," "I am not implying anything Marcus, I am just trying to ensure I have all the facts, to help me find your daughter. And as I said at the beginning, I apologise if anything I say causes you offence," "Yes, yes that's Ok, I understand. I appreciate you are only doing your job, but I assume you are not treating us as suspects." "I very much doubt that Marcus."

"Now what about Alex. How long has he worked for you?" "Just over two years," "Where did he come from?" "He came from Poland with an excellent reference from the Chairman of a shipyard in Gdansk," "Have you ever had cause to be angry with him or have a row with him," "No, never. He is extremely polite and an excellent driver. I know he took an anti-kidnap driving course and I feel completely safe with him. I am also very happy to allow him to drive Stephanie and Klara." "I will obviously check, but are you aware if has he ever been involved with the police?" "Not to my knowledge," "Does he do drugs?" "Again, not to my knowledge, and he would be instantly dismissed if I found out that he does," "Right, thank you. Let's talk about Izzy," "How long have you known her?" "She joined us in the first week of January," said Stephanie. "Sorry, of course, you did say that earlier. How did she get the job?" Marcus stepped in "I knew her father from a case he had defended for me, and we were chatting after the case and I happened to mention that we would be looking for a nanny after Christmas. Our previous nanny was leaving to get married. He thought his daughter would be interested and would ask her. Steph interviewed her over the phone and we met her for the first time in January," "Is she good with Klara and does Klara like her?" "Yes, they seem to get on like a house on fire," replied Stephanie "This may seem like a strange question, but were Izzy and Alex having an affair?" Stephanie thought for a moment, then "Well," she replied "Alex is a handsome man and I could easily see him breaking a few hearts, and Izzy is a young attractive girl, if somewhat naive. It wouldn't surprise me if there was some attraction between them, but I have not seen any evidence that they were sleeping together. Alex has his accommodation above the garage and Izzy has her room in the house. They do work long hours, so the opportunities would be limited, but she has only been with us for six weeks, I wouldn't think it possible in such a short time." "We were almost engaged after six weeks darling," laughed Marcus and Stephanie smiled at him. It was the first time they had managed to smile since Klara disappeared. The answers all seemed reasonable to Cadieux and it appeared to him highly unlikely that Alex and Izzy had plotted together to kidnap Klara, but where were they. And if Klara had been kidnapped, why no ransom demand, although it may be still a little early.

"I think we should also consider a press conference later this afternoon. I would suggest the local and national TV stations and all of the local and international newspapers. Would you be willing," "Of course, I would do anything you feel is necessary," It was Marcus who replied, but Cadieux said "It would be better if her mother was to speak, it seems to have more impact with the public, that is if you are up to it Stephanie," "Definitely, I'll do anything to help bringing her home," "I will set it up for later today. Thank you for your time and patience. Please try not to worry. We will do everything we can to get your little girl back safe and sound. Here is my card. If you think of anything else, or have any further information or any questions please do not hesitate to call me. Any time, day or night. I must now get back to my department, get my officers set up with their enquiries and organise the press conference. I will send a lady officer to stay with you, to help in any way, and to be your direct contact with me. And again, I apologise if my questions have caused you any offence," "Is there anything we should be doing Capitaine, should we offer a reward," Stephanie asked. "Not at present perhaps, but if there are no leads then maybe later, and thank you for being so frank with your answers," and with that Cadieux left them with their worries.

Stephanie said "It's all very well him saying try not to worry. I'm sure he hasn't had one of his children kidnapped." "You're right of course, but he is trying to be positive, and we must try to do the same. Perhaps you should let your parents know what has happened. You wouldn't want them to find out from the media." "I'll call them now," and a few moments later, "Hi Daddy, I'm afraid we have a problem here. Klara is missing," Stephanie then filled her father in on what had happened over the last 15 or so hours. She had to pause on several occasions being overcome with emotion. "If there is anything I can do, or any pressure I can bring to bear, please let me know," Rutherford replied. "I still have some contacts from when I worked in Germany, and some were in the French police departments, oh, and there was a politician who I think is now quite high up in the government there, Dominique de Villepin, so if you think this Cadieux guy isn't up to the job, let me know." "Thank you, Daddy, but he does seem to know what he is doing at present. He asked an awful lot of questions; some were quite personal. I will keep you up to date with any developments," "Darling, Police Officers are not noted for their sensitivity. I'm sure Marcus will be able to handle things perfectly well, but if you need me to come over, I'll be on the next plane." "Yes Daddy, Marcus is completely in charge, and when we get Klara back, perhaps we will come over to see you both. Bye, love to Mummy," to Marcus, Stephanie said "Daddy has offered his help if we need it. I said we were okay at present and that you had everything under control." "I don't know about that; I feel completely out of my depth." "Are you alright? I know losing your father last year was very upsetting for you. I know you were very close to your father, and you must miss him terribly, and now this. Don't be afraid to ask me for help if you need it." They hugged each other. "At least we have each other to help us through this, and I do love you Steph, dearly," and Stephanie, clinging tightly to her husband, wept.

Chapter 11

Cadieux returned to the Chamonix police station in Rue la Mollard, where he had ordered an incident room to be set up. He addressed his team that were assembled there. "Ladies and Gentlemen, we have what appears to be a very serious incident to deal with. Hopefully it may turn out to be nothing, but we must be prepared for all eventualities. Following a report of missing persons to Major Guillaume of the Police Municipale, I have interviewed Marcus and Stephanie Meier who were here on holiday with their daughter, nanny and chauffeur. There are three people missing. They were supposed to be back at their chalet in Chamonix yesterday afternoon after a trip to Annecy. They are an almost three year-old little girl, Klara, a nineteen-year-old English nanny, Izzy, and a twenty-eight-year-old Polish chauffeur, Alex. There are no reports of their car being involved in an accident and all hospitals have been contacted without success. The parents are intending to be present at a press conference later today. The obvious line of enquiry is one of kidnap, but there is no ransom demand as yet, could be a little early perhaps, and no contact from whoever has Klara.

There are several possibilities. One is that all three have been kidnapped by persons as yet unknown. If that is the case then the chauffeur Alex and the nanny Izzy may be in danger. A second possibility is that either Alex, or Izzy, or both together, have abducted Klara, and that they will issue a ransom demand soon. If it is Alex on his own, there is a possibility that Izzy may be in danger, and for the benefit of political correctness, if it is Izzy that has taken Klara then Alex may be in danger. The other worry is that whatever has happened, the little girl Klara may be in danger. The parents are a wealthy couple, and the father is a respected scientist who owns his own research company in Lausanne. A tracker fitted to the car developed a fault recently. It was reported to Marcus Meier by the chauffeur Alex just before this holiday. Was that tracker deliberately broken? If so by whom. We also only have the Meier's word as to when they went missing. This needs to be confirmed in the timeline. I have sent the full details of the car and the missing persons to your mobile phones. All leave is cancelled for the time being and overtime has been approved. First priority is to find the car. We have the make and registration number and that has been circulated. The Police Municipale and Gendarmerie Nationale are keeping a lookout for the car and occupants, and Interpol have been notified.

Your individual enquiry responsibilities are as follows: Officer Benoit, you are our victim liaison officer, go to the chalet and be with the parents. Be with them 24/7 and give them any support you can, but also keep your eyes and ears open, and report anything suspicious back to me immediately. I feel it is highly unlikely that the parents are involved, but we cannot rule anything out and they may mention something that they have forgotten to tell me in my interview. Also please check and confirm all the details from my interview with them and the initial report from Major Guillaume.

Laurent, take Fournier with you to Annecy and see if they were there." Lieutenant Pierre Laurent was the senior detective under Capitaine Cadieux. He was an experienced detective of many years working on major crimes and was mentoring Fournier a relatively new detective to the team. Laurent was a tall man with a mass of silver-grey hair that he was always brushing away from his eyes. He kept himself fit by going to the police gym three times a week. Fabian Fournier was 27 years old and had recently been appointed as a detective. He was also tall, but with short dark hair, a ready smile and a quick wit. He was learning a lot from his more experienced colleague, but was also able to bring a fresh insight into a situation. "Who saw them and when? Build up a timeline of their movements and try to find out the last time they were seen, and by whom. Also, a text was sent by Alex to Marcus at 4.48 p.m. yesterday saying they were held up in Annecy, due to an accident. Check with the local police that that is correct and what was the exact time of the delay.

Bertrand, you and Girard set up a phone tap and monitor calls and text messages to all four of the mobile phones and the number in the chalet. Any contact, inform me immediately. Dubois, look into Alex's background, what is his employment history before Marcus. Has he got a criminal record, does he have criminal friends, or even enemies? Does he have a drug problem, Marcus Meier says not, speak to our drugs team, see if he is on their radar. Same thing Rousseau, for Izzy, and look into her parents. They got her the job here. Have they got anything to do with it? They are apparently lawyers, but that's no guarantee. We've all come across bent lawyers before. Also, check if Alex and Izzy are having an affair. The Meier's don't believe so, but see if you can confirm it. Oh, and Dubois, check on the faulty tracker. When was it reported to the garage and booked in for repair? Marcus Meier doesn't drive the vehicle often. Try to confirm the last time either he or Stephanie Meier drove the car. See if you can obtain any history of the tracker," "I think that is only possible from the onboard computer sir, but I will check," "Also, will you organise a team from the Gendarmerie to look at any CCTV footage available from the area. Start with Chamonix and try to track their movements, presumably towards Annecy. Liaise with Laurent on what he finds out in Annecy. If they did actually go there, spread the CCTV search to there," "Yes sir,"

"Finally, Lamy and Poirier, you have the most delicate task. Stephanie and Marcus themselves. They appear to have an alibi for the time of the disappearance, but they could have organised the whole thing. Despite their protestations that they love each other, there may be some friction with Marcus working long, very long hours. Is that true, or is he having an affair with a member of his staff or someone else and using work as a cover. Could provide a motive. Again, none of this seems likely, but we must eliminate them from our enquiries. What are Stephanie's movements. Does she play tennis, do yoga? Is she a member of a gym? Does she have any personal one on one training sessions? Could she be playing away and Marcus has found out? Again, a possible motive, however unlikely.

Lefevre, you are our computer genius. Look at the accounts of Marcus and his company, see if there is anything suspicious, it is unlikely, but you never know. Any large or regular payments from his accounts which cannot be assigned to invoices. And I would also like you to compile a timeline from the results of all of the enquires. Create a folder on the police intranet for all documents relating to this operation, and provide access to all officers assigned to it. Let's hope all of this is unnecessary, and they all turn up safe and sound, but leave no stone unturned. Any questions?" Silence and shaking of heads. "No? Go to it," The room cleared and the detectives began their work.

Benoit went straight to her flat and collected a change of clothes and toiletries as she would be with Marcus and Stephanie for the duration of the operation 24 hours a day. This was something she had done on a couple of occasions and found being able to support distressed persons very satisfying. Laurent and Fournier went to their car to drive to Annecy. Bertrand started making arrangements with the technical department for telephone monitoring equipment to be sent to the chalet while Girard contacted the mobile phone providers for information. Lefevre went back to his desk, logged on to his computer, created a timeline template ready for the input of data from the teams, posted it onto a new folder for the operation and started researching the accounts of Marcus, his company, and Stephanie. Dubious had the list of Alex's contacts, most of which had telephone numbers and started making calls, and Rousseau logged on to the internet to look into the family Hunter-Smythe, and called the British Police in Sussex for a background check on the family. Cadieux called the press office and asked them to set up the press conference for later that day and to make sure local and national television were represented.

Chapter 12

Daniel took the child outside and encouraged her to play in the snow. Lizzie joined them, and they built a lovely little snowman, well, little, it was larger than the girl, and they put one of Daniels woolly hats on its head and a piece of carrot for his nose, found some black stones for eyes and coat buttons. After a while they came back into the van, made a warm milky chocolate drink for the child, coffee for themselves and warmed themselves by the gas fire. "I'm not sure what we can give her to eat. I assume she is able, to eat adult food but in much smaller amounts," said Lizzie. "I would think so," replied Daniel, "but there is very little we can do until we can get out of this snow drift. We don't have snow chains and I don't have a shovel," "She does seem okay at the moment" said Lizzie, "She played quite happily in the snow. I would have thought she'd be more traumatised seeing her parents killed like that, although maybe she doesn't realise they were dead. It was quite dark after the crash and she can't have seen much," Daniel said "The sooner we can get to a police station and hand her over the better," "She's probably only two or three and doesn't seem to understand us or what has happened," "She may be French, perhaps German or even Swiss," said Daniel. "See if she can tell you her name,"

So, Lizzie sat the girl on her knee and cuddled her in and said slowly, "My name is Lizzie, his name is Daniel, what is your name?" The child looked at her blankly, her eyes wide open, then buried her head on Lizzies chest. Trying again she'd said, "Me, Lizzie, Him, Daniel, You?". Again nothing. Lizzie pointed to herself, "Lizzie" and pointing to Daniel said "Daniel". Then pointing to the child said "You?". The girl looked at them both, smiled shyly and said, "Klara" "Klara, that's a nice name, how old are you, Klara?" No answer. "Two, Three, Four?"
More silence and blank looks. "Where do you live Klara?" Silence again. "Are you from France, or Germany or Switzerland?" Nothing. "I don't think she'll understand countries Lizzie," "No probable not, but worth a try. Perhaps I'll try a nursery rhyme,"
She started with

"*Bah bah black sheep have you any wool,*
yes sir, yes sir, three bags full.
One for the master, and one for the dame,
and one for the little boy who lives down the lane,"
"Do you know that one Klara," No response. "Perhaps I'll try Mary
had a little lamb,"
"*Mary had a little lamb,*
it's fleece as white as snow,
and everywhere that Mary went,
the lamb was sure to go"
No response. "Okay, what about Little Miss Muffett,"
"*Little Miss Muffett sat on a tuffet,*
Eating her curds and whey;
There came a big spider,
And sat down beside her,
And frightened Miss Muffett away,"
Klara then started playing with her fingers and sang a little rhyme,
not in English, not in a tune, but singing, well more reciting, quietly.
"*Das ist der Daumen*
der schüttelt die Pflaumen,
der hebt sie auf,
der trägt sie nach Haus,
und der Kliene isst sie alle auf,"
"That is nice Klara, who sings that?" asked Lizzie. "Izzy" said Klara
"Izzy, is that your mummy?" Klara looked blank. Lindsey tried again.
"Izzy, mummy?" Klara said "Izzy, Manny" "I think she said her
mummy is called Izzy", she said to Daniel, and to Klara, "Daddy?"
And Klara said "Daddy". When Lizzie started to sing Little Miss
Muffet again, Klara sang her little rhyme.
"*Das ist der Daumen*
der schüttelt die Pflaumen,
der hebt sie auf,
der trägt sie nach Haus,
und der Kliene isst sie alle auf,"

"That has to be German" Daniel said. "I wish I had taken German instead of French," "Me too, sounds German doesn't it, didn't think of going on holiday to Germany, thought mainly of France or Spain," "That's a lovely song Klara? Does mummy sing that to you," asked Lizzie? "Izzy," said Klara "Izzy sings it, Is Izzy your mummy?" asked Lizzie "Izzy Manny" "What is your daddy's name?" "Daddy," "She obviously doesn't know her parent's names," whispered Daniel, "and I don't think she realises her parents have died," "No, probably not, but at least we know her name now," replied Lizzie, "I'm getting hungry, think I'd better make some lunch. Would you like something to eat Klara?" No answer, but a big smile on Klara's face said it all.

Lizzie cut the crusts off some bread and made little soldiers, soft boiled an egg and helped Klara to eat it. Klara also had a little pâté on another piece of bread. Lizzie made their lunch of pâté, bread and ham and cheese, and a couple of small bottles of beer, while Klara had a glass of milk. They had some fruit yogurts for afterwards which Klara loved. "How far was it to the village do you think", asked Lizzie. "Couple of miles perhaps. This afternoon I'll see if I can get back up to the road, and then I might be able to walk to the village. I don't think we'll be able to get the van out for another two or three days at the earliest. The snow is too deep". "If we're lucky. I just wish we had brought a mobile" moaned Lizzie. "At least we would have been able to get some help". "Yup, I agree. That was a big mistake. Still, can't do anything about that now. Just have to make the best of it".

Chapter 13

Marcus and Stephanie were driven to Rue la Mollard where a room had been prepared for the press conference. The room was large but was packed with reporters, photographers and television crews. There was a table at the front with three chairs and three pitchers of water with glasses. There was a display board behind the table which had the logo of the Police Nationale emblazoned on it. Lights and television cameras had been erected at the rear of the room, and in front of them four rows of chairs for the journalists and photographers. Cadieux led Marcus and Stephanie into the room, and the TV lights were turned up to full power. The photographers, well prepared, fired off several pictures each, trying to get the best picture for publication. It was just as well that cameras were now digital and film was not required, much easier to dispose of poor pictures. Stephanie, fashionably dressed in trousers and a cashmere jumper with a scarf tied around her neck sat in the middle chair flanked by Marcus in a sports jacket with a polo necked jumper and chinos, holding her hand tightly, and Cadieux, in a navy two-piece suit, blue shirt and a colourful tie, who opened the proceedings.

"I am Capitaine Antoine Cadieux of the Police Nationale, and I am the officer in charge of a search for three missing persons including a nearly three-year-old little girl, Klara Meier. Klara was last seen almost 24 hours ago in the company of her nanny, Isabella Hunter-Smythe, known as Izzy, a nineteen-year-old English girl, and Alexsander Lewandowski, a twenty-eight-year-old Polish chauffeur known as Alex. The chauffeur has worked for the Meier's for about two years and the nanny about 6 weeks. We are becoming increasingly concerned about their whereabouts, and the child's welfare. The family were on holiday here, the parents were skiing yesterday at Chamonix and the three missing persons were apparently taking a trip to Annecy. We are asking for the public's help in finding them. Photographs of the car, a black Mercedes E55AMG and all three persons will be handed out following this press conference. I would now like to introduce Klara's mother, Stephanie Meier, who would like to say something, following which I will be happy to take questions"

Stephanie had obviously been crying, she was pale and drawn and her eyes were red. She had tried to brush her hair and make herself presentable, but still had the haggard look she had had since the morning. She looked into the bright television lights as more flashguns were set off by the photographers. "Please whoever has my little girl, will they please hand her over to the nearest policeman. No questions asked. Let her come home to us. We love her and miss her. I'm sure she is lonely and frightened and needs to be back with her Mummy and Daddy," Stephanie then broke down weeping and was comforted by Marcus who was also on the verge of tears.

Questions were then fired at the Capitaine. "How large is the team searching for Klara," "My team is currently 16, but we have the assistance of the Gendarme and Police Municipale. There will be no limit to the number of officers we will be able to use in our enquiries," "Has Interpol been notified," "Yes, along with all airports and ports, and photographs circulated," "Have you any positive leads as to who might have taken Klara," "We are pursuing a number of different possibilities," "Are the nanny and chauffeur considered suspects," "At this time, we have not eliminated anyone from our enquiries," "Has a reward for information been offered," "No, There …" Cadieux started to answer but Marcus stepped in, cutting him off, "Yes, we are happy to provide a reward of €50,000 for any information leading to the safe return of Klara," Stephanie smiled at him, but Cadieux remained impassive. The press conference was the major news item on all of the local channels with the photographs of all three shown prominently. Cadieux then left the press conference, a not very happy man, and returned to the incident room leaving Officer Benoit to escort Marcus and Stephanie back to their chalet.

That afternoon, Daniel made an effort to get up the track but found it very difficult. He came back to the van. "I think there is a little bit of a thaw going on, I'll give it another try in the morning, if it doesn't snow again tonight. Would you like me to make supper, or let me hold her while you make supper?" Daniel said. Lizzie handed Klara over and made supper. "I'd rather not have food poisoning," she laughed. Daniel sat Klara on his lap and tried to play with her. He again started saying the Little Miss Muffett nursery rhyme, but Klara played with her fingers again and sang her own little nursery rhyme

"Das ist der Daumen
der schüttelt die Pflaumen,
der hebt sie auf,
der trägt sie nach Haus,
und der Kliene isst sie alle auf,"

Daniel said "I think 'das ist der' means 'this is the', and 'und der' means 'and this'. I don't understand anything else, but playing with her fingers, I wonder if it is something like a German version of This Little Piggy Went to Market," "You could be right. She always seems to be playing with her fingers when she sings it. I'll try that," So Daniel took Klara's hand and spoke

This little piggy went to market
This little piggy stayed home
This little piggy had roast beef
This little piggy had none
And this little piggy cried wee wee wee all the way home

And at the same time tickling Klara under her arms. Klara giggled, so Daniel played the game again. Klara did not join in with the rhyme but giggled every time. "Well, I think she enjoys the rhyme," said Daniel "and I think she does understand a little English, which is promising isn't it," Lizzie made supper from some chicken breasts and a cheese sauce mix with some vegetables and chips. Klara loved the chips, ate a few small pieces of chicken and some of the vegetables.

After supper, they settled Klara down for the night and, accompanied by large glasses of wine, tried to relax with a game of Yahtzee, but they kept worrying about how soon they would be able to get Klara back to safety. Daniel wanted to try to make an early start the next day, so they turned in at half past nine. Klara woke up crying around 2 am, so Lizzie brought her into their bed and after a little while Klara, clinging tightly to Lizzie, stopped crying and went back to sleep.

Chapter 14

Cadieux had had a restless night. This case was his bête noire. He had dealt with, and solved, several murders, with the perpetrators now behind bars, but the abduction of a child was the one that brought back his worst nightmares. As a young detective he had been involved in the kidnap of a small boy, held for a ransom of a million francs. His senior officer had, in his opinion, made several mistakes, and the result was that the ransom was paid, the kidnappers escaped and the boy was found dead. The post-mortem revealed that he had been alive after the payment of the ransom and Cadieux could still see the body of the boy lying on the slab in the morgue in his mind's eye. It was, in fact, the first post-mortem he had attended. He was haunted by the looks on the parents faces when they were told the news that their only sons body had been found and would never forget the anguish he had felt. He had promised himself then that such an event would never happen on his watch if he could prevent it. His wife Marie had tried her best to console him, and eventually he managed a few short hours of troubled sleep.

He arrived at his desk at 6.30 the next morning feeling drained but two strong cups of coffee later he had read through all of the communiqués from the various police forces who had been searching for the car and the three missing persons. There had been no reported sightings and he was concerned that the offer of a reward would cause more work for his team dealing with timewasters and glory seekers. By 7 o'clock his team had assembled and he gave them the negative results of the reports from the other police forces and Interpol. Cadieux then went round the table for their updates.

"Laurent & Fournier you were looking at Annecy," Laurent spoke up "Yes, they were in Annecy sir. We showed the photographs around and several shopkeepers saw them. At present the last one to see them was at the Les Glacier des Alps around half past two, where they bought three ice creams. They had seemed like a normal happy family. They walked away holding hands with the little girl between them apparently skipping along quite happily," "Mm..., maybe Marcus and Stephanie could be right, but keep an open mind," "As for the delay sir, there was a fatal accident at 2.50 p.m. on the outskirts of Annecy leading towards Chamonix. It was at a crossroads and the area was closed for over an hour while the fire department had to cut out the driver. The area was in chaos, then there was another accident closing the D909 around tenpast four." "That seems to corroborate the text message then. Maybe he isn't involved, but keep checking," "Marcus booked a taxi at 5.22 p.m. in Chamonix which took them back to the chalet, arriving at" Laurent consulted his notebook "5.47," "Again, that agrees with what Marcus has said," "That's it for the moment sir," "Bertrand & Girard phones?" "Nothing yet sir, all phones have traces on them, no contacts at all. The mobiles are not switched on at the moment, so no way of tracking their location. The phone companies have agreed to send us a transcript of any text messages, but they are not instantaneous. Could take anything from half an hour to four hours," "I hope that's not going to be a problem."

"Lefevre, Accounts please," "Still ploughing through sir, but nothing suspicious at all as yet. As you said sir, he is well respected in the research community. Has been in business in Lausanne since 1997, came from America where he worked for Merck. He seems too good to be true. Always paid his taxes and his returns are always in on time. I drove over to Lausanne and interviewed the staff. His employees speak highly of him as a boss, although he does come across as very focused and driven and has a short fuse if things aren't done correctly, or to his satisfaction. Other than that, the staff seem to enjoy working there. No one had a bad word to say about him, no one has left the company for any reason for over two years and they all received a substantial pay rise and bonus in December,"

"Wonder if he wants a security man," interjected Fournier.

Laughter echoed around the incident room and Cadieux chuckled. "Get in line Fournier. Dubois, what about Alex"

"Yes sir, again seems to be a perfect employee. I telephoned his previous employer, the chairman of a Gdansk shipyard who had lost his licence due to a drink driving conviction, who gave him a glowing reference. Alex was an excellent chauffeur, polite, smart and never found wanting. Stayed late when required. Always prepared to go the extra mile," The room again collapsed into laughter at the pun, easing the tension a little. "Okay, okay, settle down," But Cadieux was smiling. It was always good to enjoy a little humour in an intense situation. He had a good team and was very proud of the way they worked together, despite the often long unsocial hours when the team was handed a case such as this. "And the tracker on the car was reported faulty to the main Mercedes dealers garage Mercedes Reidy in Lausanne on the 17th February at 11.35 am. It is due to go in for investigation on March 9th," "Ok but it could still have been deliberately broken. Anything on the tracker history," "No sir, it is as I thought, the history is on the cars computer memory, so when we find the car...," "Right thank you Dubois,"

"Rousseau anything on Izzy?" "Yes sir, well actually no sir, nothing. Sad story. Very clever girl. Three A stars in her A levels. Due to go to Oxford University to study law. In her gap year. Returned from Africa last Christmas volunteering for a charity getting water to villages. Family is devastated that she is missing. Parents are very well-known lawyers and in fact the father Humphrey Hunter-Smythe is a Q.C. Can't believe that she was involved sir," "Okay, doesn't look likely. I don't have her down as a criminal mastermind, but you never know, so we won't rule her out just yet."

"Lamy & Poirier, Marcus & Stephanie," It was Poirier who answered "Sir, Stephanie comes from a very, very wealthy family, so doesn't need money. Marcus is also wealthy, although not in the same league as his in-laws, very well thought of in the pharmaceutical research industry. He seems to be completely clean. His mother died when he was quite young and his father was a pharmacist, but passed away last year. There is no obvious reason why either of them would need to organise this. There is also no evidence at present that either of them is playing away from home. When Marcus says he is at work, he is at work. There is a card entry system at his research company and it is state of the art. He is obviously very concerned about security. The door entry log shows he is a workaholic. Stephanie has a social circle which is entirely comprised of women, so no gentlemen friends, and unless she has changed sides...... She doesn't have a personal trainer, yoga teacher or tennis coach. Stephanie's father is the CEO of an international merchant bank. The family lived in Germany for many years where Stephanie was born, before his appointment as CEO. Lives in New York, which is where Marcus and Stephanie met. Has many influential friends, including incidentally the French Interior Minister," "No pressure then," it was Fournier again with the remark. "I am aware of that Fournier, thank you." "From their friends I have talked to, they are very much a close couple with a wide social network, and liked by them all. I very much doubt their involvement sir." "Thank you Poirier, I tend to agree with you, but….. Ladies and Gentlemen, thank you for your efforts thus far, but keep on looking, keep digging, doing what you are good at. Unfortunately, the father, Marcus Meier jumped in at the press conference and has offered a substantial reward for information. I regret that this will increase our workload so I have asked the local Gendarmerie for some additional resources to man the phones, however amongst all of the dross, we may turn up a nugget or two. We must stay vigilant. We still have not received any ransom demand, so we are still in the dark. Let me know the instant you find out any further information. I shall liaise with the parents and be back at H.Q. later today," and as he left the incident room, the phones started ringing.

There had been a light snowfall overnight but the sun was bright in a cloudless sky and it was quite warm. Daniel looked outside and decided to wait until the afternoon to try to reach the road. They played in the snow with Klara in the morning and tried singing the nursery rhymes again, particularly This Little Piggy. Klara responded again with her own rhyme. "That's a lovely song Klara, can I sing it with you" asked Lizzie. They sang together, but Lizzie, despite her best efforts. could not get the German pronunciation right at all. Daniel chimed in as well, but he was even worse and made Klara giggle, especially when he pulled funny faces. Klara had not cried at all today, so Lizzie was feeling somewhat relieved. After lunch, they settled Klara down for a nap whilst Daniel made another attempt to reach the road. He had managed to pull a branch from a tree and used it as a walking stick. This helped him climb the 400 or so metres up the track and reach the road.

Chapter 15

There were a few tyre tracks in the snow-covered road, so he was able to walk quite easily. No vehicles passed him on his half a mile

or so walk before he reached the village, well it was not quite a village, more a hamlet, and in the small store he saw some newspapers in a rack. The shopkeeper was sitting behind the counter, a cigarette in his mouth, reading one of the papers. They were all in French of course but he called on his schoolboy language skills to read the headlines. What he saw shook him to the core.
ENFANT KIDNAPPE
la police recherche une fillette de trois ans kidnappée par sa nounou et son complice.
Daniel was stunned. He couldn't make out all of the words, but he knew enough to understand that police were looking for kidnappers. He took the paper to the counter and the shopkeeper gave him his change but looked long and hard at Daniel. Having bought the paper he hurried as fast as he could back to the camper van.

Getting back into the van he said "Lizzie, I think we have a problem". They spread the newspaper out onto the dining table and tried to decipher the French article between them. Lizzie said "All we have to do is take her to a police station, and hand her in," Daniel wasn't convinced. "I'm not so sure, we don't speak the language that well, and we can't really explain why we have had her for almost three days. The police, and this Capitaine Cadieux, are looking for kidnappers and we could be arrested for kidnapping Klara," "I'm sure they would believe us. I mean it's not as if we have issued a ransom demand, is it?" "Maybe so, I just don't fancy trying to explain in my pigeon French why we have had her so long," "Would we not be able to see the British ambassador, wouldn't they help us." "I just don't know." "I mean we've probably saved her life, that must count for something, perhaps we could just drop her off at the village shop, and go back home." "Then the shopkeeper would have the Gendarme looking for us in a matter of minutes. He was giving me some funny looks as I was looking through the papers. We probably wouldn't get past Annecy,"

"Surely the longer we keep her, the worse it will be to try to explain." "You may be right; we just have to try to fathom out what is the best course of action." For the rest of the day and late into the evening, they thought about what to do. Discussed various options, but couldn't come to a conclusion. What were the alternatives. What were they to do?

What now.

What next.

Chapter 16

In the early evening Cadieux called again on Marcus and Stephanie. They were sitting close together, Marcus with his arm around Stephanie who was pale and had obviously been weeping. Marcus was also dishevelled and red eyed. Benoit brought coffee in for them all. "I'm afraid I have no news as yet. Our enquiries are proceeding satisfactorily, but we have no positive responses." Marcus found his voice, "Capitaine Cadieux, how can you say enquiries are proceeding satisfactorily when you have had no responses and haven't found Klara." "Of course, you are quite right Monsieur Meier," responded Cadieux defensively, "It is most unsatisfactory to not have anything positive to report," and thinking quickly said "what I meant to say was, we have eliminated several avenues with our enquiries and we are able to focus on some more productive lines of enquiry. My teams are working diligently around the clock, searching for any sign of the car and occupants and any financial traffic with the bank accounts or credit cards of Alex and Izzy. When their mobile phones are switched on, we will be tracking their location. There has been no sighting since they left Annecy and there have been no transactions on their credit cards. Interpol and neighbouring police forces have been notified and whilst there is no sighting as yet we are confident that we will find Klara and bring her back to you safe and well," "Is that all you can do?" cried Stephanie, "What else would you have me do, Madame Meier. I know you are worried and frightened for Klara; I assure you we are doing everything possible to locate your daughter," "I want her home with me, just find her please," she cried. As he was leaving, he checked with Benoit, "Anything suspicious?" "No sir, they are distraught, but just comforting each other. They seem very close. The only call they made was to Stephanie's father," "Okay, thank you. Keep watching and listening," "Sir,"

Lizzie made supper for them all while Daniel played with Klara, although they didn't have any toys for her. "I think we should get something for Klara to play with," Daniel said "as soon as we get out of the snow, we'll find something for her." They had bought several meals for two from the Carrefour delicatessen in Annecy and had them in the small camper freezer. Lizzie chose one, but added extra vegetables and potatoes, not that Klara ate an awful lot. "If we can't get the camper out of here and it becomes necessary, I'll have to walk into the village and buy more food," said Daniel. "We're OK for two or three more days," replied Lizzie "we have three more main meals, bread, eggs, baked beans, cooked meats and we've even got another three cartons of long-life milk, so there's no urgency yet." After dinner Daniel sat Klara on his knee and she cuddled in to him while he made up a story about a little girl who fell asleep and was rescued by a prince. Lizzie thought the story was full of holes, but Klara seemed to enjoy it even if they weren't sure she understood it. "She's asleep." Lizzie whispered and carefully picked Klara up and put her in the bunk bed. "I'll have to brush up on my story telling when our kids need them." Lizzie was surprised at his comment "Do you think we'll be having any?" Actually, Daniel was also surprised at what he had said. "Only if you really want them," smiled Daniel. "Certainly not until I've qualified, and are you sure that this relationship is what you want?" "I'm very sure, but I fully agree with you about you becoming a doctor. I think you'll make an excellent doctor, but I would like to spend the rest of my life with you." "Is that a proposal?" "Perhaps it may be too early for a formal proposal, but I do love you." "We hardly know each other" "I wouldn't put it quite like that." "You know what I mean," and playfully punched his arm. "Well, yes I suppose this could be just infatuation, but you're the only girl that has ever made me feel this way, and I'm happy for it to continue." "This has come as a bit of a shock Daniel, I think I do love you, yes, I do, but I think we need to take more time over this." "I may have been a little bit premature, but I did mean what I said." "Does this mean were engaged?" "Only if you say yes." "Well then," Lizzie though for a moment, then "Yes." "Klara you're a witness," pulled Lizzie to him and kissed her, but Klara just lay there gently sleeping with her eyes tightly shut.

Chapter 17

Daniel and Lizzie had both spent a disturbed night excitedly dreaming about if they were actually engaged or not and not so excitedly thinking about their predicament, and a clear-cut resolution had not presented itself to either. The weather was turning milder, but there were still some snow flurries and it was still not possible to get the camper van out onto the road. "I'll go back to the village and get a bus into Annecy, and try to get an English paper to read all about it," Daniel announced at breakfast time. "I think it should take me three or four hours. Will you be okay on your own with Klara?". "Yes, you know I will, she's no bother now, were getting on like a house on fire, and she's teaching me German. Not that she knows it of course," Daniel, once again wrapped up against the worst of the weather, managed to get back up the track to the road, set off for the village and found there was no bus service to Annecy. What kind of one-horse town is this he thought to himself? He went to the shop where he had bought yesterday's paper, the shopkeeper still giving him funny looks, (well in Daniels furtive mind anyway) but the shop still did not have any

English newspapers. He asked if there was a taxi from the village. The shopkeeper gave him a number and pointed to a payphone at the end of his shop. Daniel called for a taxi, which arrived in about five minutes.

In Annecy he noticed a very large police presence, most carrying guns, his mind was working overtime, and he felt that all of them were looking at him. He found a shop selling English newspapers, bought one, and was astonished at what he read. He went to a DIY store and bought a shovel and a pair of snow chains. As he came out of the shop, Daniel was looking for a taxi when he was stopped by a policeman carrying a gun. He felt himself go pale and thought his legs would give way. "Excusez-moi monsieur à quoi sert la pelle" The officer said. Daniel concentrated hard, and in his best schoolboy French said "je ne parle pas très bien le français. Pouvez-vous parler anglais". "Why do you .. erm .. require the .. er .. shovel," "Erm.. my car is stuck in the snow and erm... I have also bought snow chains," said Daniel showing the chains to the officer. "D'accord, au revoir meilleurs voeux avec ta voiture," (*Okay, goodbye best wishes with your car*)

Daniel breathed a huge sigh of relief after the officer had gone, flagged down another taxi and went back to Thones, being dropped outside the village store. He went into the store, where he was sure the shopkeeper was still giving him a strange look, bought a few groceries, and, loaded down, walked back to the camper van. He'd been gone four-and-a-half hours. He was starving and ready for some lunch and then got down to telling Lizzie about his brush with the gendarme. "I was sure he could tell I knew where Klara was," "Guilty conscience," "I suppose so". They then read the front-page article for the details of the reported kidnapping. The police were apparently looking for the chauffeur and nanny, who were believed to have abducted the daughter of a wealthy German businessman, and granddaughter of an American multi-millionaire, but had not yet issued a ransom demand. They had disappeared in a Mercedes limousine, and the registration number, pictures of the car, chauffeur and nanny, as well as Klara, were all in the paper. The police thought that the chauffeur and nanny may have been working together, and had orchestrated the trip to Annecy to disguise their abduction. "So, the couple in the car are not Klara's parents," said Lizzie. "Perhaps that is why Klara is not so upset. Of course, Klara said Izzy, Manny, I thought she said Mammy, but she must have meant Nanny." Interpol had been notified and all EU police forces were on the lookout for the car and its occupants.

There was a reward for any information leading to the safe return of their daughter, Klara. "A reward, that's great", Lizzie said, "We can hand her in and collect the reward," "I'm not so sure," said Daniel. "Nobody knows who we are, where we are, or even in fact if we even exist," "But €50,000, is that not reward enough?," "Is ok by it could be a lot more." "What about that policeman in Annecy". "Oh, he will have forgotten all about me by now," Daniel was quiet for several minutes, then, "What if we were to issue a ransom demand ourselves?" "You can't be serious," "Just think of it. They are obviously a very wealthy family and we wouldn't be greedy, just enough to set both of us up, pay off your university fees, and some left over. My computer game is just about ready to go to market which I could then afford to do. We would just have to work out the details. Obviously, we wouldn't hurt, or even threaten to hurt Klara. I couldn't do that, that wouldn't be right, but this could be an opportunity to set is on the road to financial security for life. We've been handed a golden opportunity. It's up to us if we are brave enough to take it," "Or stupid enough," Lizzie was astonished at Daniels idea. There was no way she would agree to that. It was ridiculous to even consider it. "No Daniel, that is not on, I'm surprised at you even suggesting it. No way."

Chapter 18

No way…. No, no way…… Lizzie was shocked at the idea…… actually she was more shocked that she was now thinking about it, now considering it…No, it was ridiculous…. It would never work….. It wouldn't work…… It couldn't work…… could it?….. but then again, …. maybe it could. The more she thought about it, the more the possibility began to make some kind of sense. Maybe Daniel had something. Nobody knew who they were or where they were. They had no connection to the family. They could just collect the ransom and drive back to England and no one would be any the wiser. Or would they? The family were very wealthy, and we wouldn't do anything to hurt Klara. Klara would be back with her parents in a few days, and they did save her life. They deserved something for that surely. She started to convince herself that it was a good idea. It's the sort of thing her older brother would have thought of. Was she like her older brother? Worse still, would she end up like her older brother, In prison! Daniel had been sitting quietly for several minutes, obviously thinking about something, then he exclaimed, "Of course, why didn't I think of that before, they must have had mobile phones with them in the car. The batteries will be flat by now, but they would probably have had chargers with them. I'll see if I can find the car again and get their mobiles. We could use them to contact the parents," "If we decide to go ahead with your hairbrained scheme" "Yes, if we do, you're thinking about it obviously." "Ok then, I'll think about it." "That's OK, we won't go ahead without your complete agreement." "I'll stay here with Klara, Daniel, and think" "Yeah, that's OK, no problem. No point us all getting cold and wet, and it is probably better she doesn't see the car again anyway, but I could murder a cup of coffee before I leave,"

So, Lizzie made him a coffee while he got dressed again in warm clothing, hat, gloves and boots and then, after drinking his coffee, he set off again, down into the valley towards the crash site. The snow hadn't relented much, in fact it was heavier now so the going was still slow, and it took an hour to find the car. He almost missed it again as it was still completely covered in snow, even thicker now, but he managed to prise open the front passenger door, and looked in the glove compartment. Sure enough, there was a mobile phone charger cable in there plugged into the cigarette lighter, but no sign of a phone. He braced himself for what he had to do next. Leaning over the body of the nanny he felt in the jacket pocket of the driver and there it was. Wow, that was the latest model of the Motorola flip phone, the Razr V3. He looked in the rear of the car and saw a handbag, obviously the nanny's handbag. Searching through it he found her mobile, this time a much older Nokia. It looked like an 8210 model to Daniel, because that is what he had at home. How he wished he hadn't been an idiot and insisted on leaving the phones at home, although if they had had their phones they would have immediately called for help after seeing the crash. He tried switching them on, but, as he thought, both were flat. Try as he may, he could not find the charging equipment for the Nokia, however one would be available at any mobile phone shop in Annecy. He pocketed the mobile phones and the charging cable, closed up the car doors again, and remembered that he had not taken off his Thinsulate gloves, so fingerprints would not be left. He stood by the car for several minutes trying to think if he had left any incriminating evidence. Satisfied that he hadn't, he started back to the van.

On his way back he thought of the ways he could plan the ransom demand. Differing scenarios running through his head. His first, and top, priority was that Klara would be returned to her parents safe and sound. That wasn't up for discussion, not that Lizzie would agree to anything else, but he couldn't dream of hurting or even threatening to hurt Klara. The second priority was that Lizzie would be kept at a safe distance. It was his idea, and he would not have

Lizzie incriminated if he could avoid it. The third priority was to decide on the amount of the ransom. It couldn't be too large, he wouldn't want to take too much, but it appeared from the newspaper that that the family were well off, and if they could afford a nanny and a chauffeur, they must be, but the ransom needed to be sufficient to set them up. The fourth priority was what form would the ransom take, cash or electronic transfer. There were advantages and disadvantages to both and he decided he would discuss the options with Lizzie when he got back to the campervan. The snow was still falling quite heavily, covering his tracks, and he was delighted when he saw the lights of the van appearing through the blizzard.

Chapter 19

Having hung his snow-covered clothes up to dry, Daniel opened up the Razr phone and removed the SIM card then put the phone on charge from the cigarette lighter in the van. Fortunately, mobile phones don't take a lot of charge from a car battery, but he had fitted a small generator and went outside and started it up to keep the camper battery topped up. After supper he sat with Lizzie to try to work out their ransom plan. He saw that the Razr phone was fully charged. He knew that mobile phones have the ability to make emergency calls without a SIM card, and as such the location could be traced if it was switched on. He decided not to power up the mobiles until a suitable time later. Daniel had read about Android Device Manager and Dr.Fone programs that were able to reset mobile phone passwords. That was something he would have to investigate.

Having read several detective novels, one mantra he remembered most of the detectives using was "follow the money". That would certainly be where the detectives would concentrate their efforts. He appreciated that there were at least a couple of dangerous times in any ransom plan. The first was when the ransom was left and the pick-up was made. The second was the release of Klara. Klara was only two or three years old and could not be left without supervision of some kind. He discussed the options with Lizzie.

His first suggestion for the ransom was to ask for cash. Unmarked used notes in small denominations seemed to be the best. Was cash the answer? Euros, Sterling or US dollars, US dollars he felt were easier to move around, low denomination, used notes. What were the problems with cash? He thought it might be difficult to travel with it in a bag or holdall. Going back on the ferry, the camper might be searched, but being a UK citizen there was little likelihood of being stopped by Customs when they returned to England. He did have to consider a safe place to hide the money so it wasn't obvious, once he had picked it up. He calculated that the money would only weigh around 4 Kg in $100 notes, and as all US dollars were the same size and weight that would double for $50 notes and be 20 Kg for $20 notes. 20 Kg was not much less than a bag of cement so that posed a problem in carrying it, both for him and Marcus. 8 Kg wasn't too heavy so perhaps $50 notes would work. $100 notes might be too easy to trace. The obvious place to hide the money was in the spaces under the seats which converted into a bed at night. But was that too obvious? Would customs search there first. Perhaps, if they were actually searching for hidden contraband, drugs even, but how would they know? Customs officers didn't always know who was bringing in drugs and a young couple in a camper van might be regarded as potential drug users. All of these concerns were raising doubts about using cash. Also, if he asked for cash, even if he demanded that the notes were unmarked and not recorded, could he be sure that the numbers of at least some of the notes, even only one, would not be recorded or marked in some way. When they tried to spend them or bank them, they could wind up arrested and in prison.

His second suggestion was an electronic banking transaction of some sort. He was extremely comfortable using electronic banking, and was already using Microsoft Money software to access his accounts online. He had looked at banking in Belize, Hong Kong and the Cayman Islands, when researching for his company and had found he could open an account remotely and in all cases their confidentiality rules were very strict. He could also open a Swiss Bank account, which he had read were very stringent on privacy, in fact the Swiss Banking Act of 1934 made it a criminal offence to disclose the name of the account holder. Minimum age for the account was 18, and he was very close to Switzerland. He could go to Switzerland and open an account but that could take time. Time which he didn't think he had, even though they did not have a deadline to return to England. He thought he could transfer money quickly from bank to bank and perhaps hide the transactions in the offshore banks. His next problem was to find a secure way to collect the ransom. He was already certain that Marcus and the police Capitaine Cadieux would be trying to arrest the kidnappers when the ransom money was picked up, so there had to be a way to create a diversion for any police interference in the ransom delivery and collection. Daniel and Lizzie talked through all of their ideas, and to be honest, none sounded completely fool proof. Daniel realised that in fact, of they proceeded with their plan, they were both going to be criminals, not something to be entered into lightly. Lizzie agreed reluctantly, very reluctantly, to go ahead with the plan, on the proviso that whatever happened, Klara would be returned unharmed to her parents, with or without the ransom. Daniel fully agreed with that and said he would surrender to the police and confess if it came to that. It was never his intention that Klara be harmed, neither would there be any threat to harm Klara, or to incriminate Lizzie, even though by helping him she was and accessory. They agreed to sleep on it and see if anything else came to mind during the night.

Chapter *20*

They woke to the sun streaming through the camper van windows and whilst Daniel made breakfast, Lizzie got Klara dressed. Daniel had thought of an improvement overnight, and explained his idea to Lizzie. She thought it was a clever amendment, so they decided to stick to their final plan, with Daniel's very subtle alteration, although Daniel said they still had to remain flexible. The ransom demand would have to be worded very carefully. "We'll need to buy two more mobiles." Daniel said "to kept in touch with each other. We'll only use their mobiles to contact the parents, and we must remove the SIM cards and switch them off so that the locations can't be traced unless we want that." So, their plan was hatched, and very nervously they put it into action. Meanwhile Klara had been playing with the scrabble tiles trying to build them into a tower and Lizzie had tried to teach her three letter words like mat, cat, dog, hen and pig with little drawings that could possibly have looked like the animals, but would take some imagination.

Daniel fitted the snow chains to the rear wheels of the camper, and as they had driven into the track, dug snow out from behind all of the wheels. He then got Lizzie to slowly drive the van backwards. She put far too much power onto the engine first time, and the wheels spun in the snow, burying the van deeper. Daniel told her to keep the revs low on the engine, dug more snow out, and asked her to try again. This time she was much better, and slowly the van pulled out of the ruts, and backwards up the track. Lizzie almost ran the van off the track and down into the ravine at one point, but a warning shout from Daniel avoided that nightmare scenario. Lizzie pulled forward, straightened up the van and then reversed back up the track. The sun had disappeared behind dark clouds, the sky looked heavy and threatening and snow had started to fall again. Daniel was concerned that if they did not get free today, they could be stuck for several more days. Twice more the wheels had to be dug out, but eventually they managed to get out onto the road, just as the snow once more turned into a blizzard. Daniel was exhausted from clearing the snow and almost collapsed onto the settee. Lizzie looked outside at the snowstorm saying "I think we just got out in time," "If this snow keeps up no one will know we've been here," replied Daniel hopefully, looking down at their disappearing tyre tracks.

Cadieux called the morning briefing to order. It was 6.30 a.m. and the team, which had now increased to 54 officers, was assembled. Cadieux called each one of his team to go over their enquiries and any results.

"Fournier, where is Laurent?" "Yes sir, Laurent is following up with a taxi driver who picked up a couple from Annecy and may have had a child with them but that is uncertain. All shopkeepers, hotels and guest houses have been visited without success. The ice cream shop appears to be the last positive sighting at around 2.45 p.m."

"Bertrand & Girard phones?"

"Still nothing sir, no contacts at all. The mobiles must be switched off as they are still not sending a signal to the masts, so we have no idea where they are at present, although the last time the phones were pinged was outside Annecy on the D909 at 17:12 on Tuesday 22nd February. We cannot get an exact location as the masts are quite a long distance apart and we haven't been able to triangulate their position," replied Bertrand "I have been through their text messages and emails and there is no trace of blackmail, or secret assignations. They seem squeaky clean sir. The most salacious is that Izzy confided in a friend that she fancied Alex like mad and thought he was gorgeous,"

"Lefevre, how is the timeline going, and their Accounts," "I have the timeline up and running and it is available on the Police Intranet. Officers have been advised as to their login details. I have finished going through all of the accounts and can confirm nothing suspicious. All expenditure is meticulously recorded against invoices or receipts. Marcus has a substantial balance in both his company and private accounts, certainly well over a million Euros combined and Stephanie has her own accounts with more than half a million Euros in her checking and savings accounts and a trust fund of 2 million US dollars. No reason to get involved in a kidnapping scam," "Thank you, Lefevre, as I thought, not the family.

Dubois, anything on Alex?" "Yes sir, Alex doesn't appear to have an email address, seeming to rely on text and social media. I have asked for a transcript of his texts and social media accounts, and they should be with me later today. His previous employer, the chairman of a Gdansk shipyard, is most concerned. He has been banned from driving again and was hoping to lure him back to Gdansk on a much higher salary. Obviously didn't learn his lesson," "Thank you. Rousseau, Izzy" "Parents are devastated. Izzy has had a couple of boyfriends, both living in England, but the British police have checked, and they both have solid alibi's for this week. Her mother did notice a change in Izzy's telephone calls. She seemed to be happier and bubblier. Whether that has anything to do with Alex, she wasn't sure. Could be of course that she was enjoying her life as a nanny instead of digging for water in Africa. No-one from her time in Africa has made any contact," "Emails? Texts? Social Media?" "Yes sir, as with Dubois I have requested transcripts and am waiting for them to arrive,"

"Poirier, Marcus & Stephanie,"
"Absolute zero Capitaine. As white as the driven snow. Not one thing I could latch onto," "I know you are doing everything possible but we need to step up our game. Think outside the box. If anyone has any bright ideas, now is the time to make a name for yourself." No one spoke. Cadieux couldn't fault any of them for their efforts and nothing appeared to have been missed, but there was no progress. He did not look forward to his meeting with Marcus and

Stephanie later this morning. Thanking his officers for their efforts, he asked them to re-double their efforts and with a sense of foreboding left for the chalet.

When Cadieux arrived at the chalet he spoke to Benoit who was also unable to add anything positive. Entering the lounge, he found Stephanie in an animated telephone conversation with her father in America. "Daddy, Capitaine Cadieux has just arrived" "Let me speak to him please." He demanded a full report of the progress in finding his granddaughter. The problem that Cadieux had, was that his officers were doing everything humanly possible, but there was just no trace of the car or its occupants. It was as if they had disappeared off the face of the earth. Cadieux explained all of his teams progress reports (other than that regarding Marcus and Stephanie) to Stephanie's father who did not seem to appreciate all of the hard work that the team were doing. "For God's sake man, just find the goddamn child and bring her home," were his parting words before slamming down the phone.

After hanging up the phone to the irate grandfather, Cadieux again apologised to Marcus, Stephanie having heard the lack of progress, had fled to her bedroom in tears again. "Marcus, I have increased my team to 54 officers, plus the combined efforts of the Gendarmerie and the Police Municipale. We're searching all of the areas within a 50 km radius of Annecy and Interpol are monitoring the rest of Europe. I am sure there will be a sighting soon or there will be contact from Alex and Izzy," "You had better hope so Cadieux, or I'll make sure you are on traffic duty for the rest of your career. You seem to be just waiting for them to contact us instead of being proactive. Do something man" he yelled "and find my daughter," and with that he stormed off to comfort Stephanie.

Cadieux appreciated that Marcus was frustrated and under a lot of stress which was causing his temper outbreak. Cadieux was also under immense pressure himself and feeling the strain, but he could not think of anything else he could possibly do. Maybe traffic duty wouldn't be so bad.

Chapter 21

Stephanie's father called the French Interior Minister Dominique de Villepin and after being put through, "Good morning, Dominique, Rutherford here, it's been a long time," "Too long Rutherford, how are you?" After exchanging a few pleasantries, each enquiring about the others families, he got down to the reason for his call. "Dominique, I have a problem which I hope you can help me with. My granddaughter is missing and one of your officers, a Capitaine Cadieux of the Police Nationale, is in charge of finding her, and things do not seem to be progressing too quickly or too well. If you could see what you can do, I would appreciate it," "Certainly Rutherford, I will make enquiries and call you back," "If you need any other resources, I am sure the American Ambassador will be able to provide any assistance. I will tell him to expect your call if required." "I have complete confidence in my officers and I am sure Capitaine Cadieux is doing everything he can, but any assistance could be useful. I will call Cadieux and get an update and call you back." "I intend flying to Paris in the next few hours to be with my daughter. Perhaps we can meet again. It's been too long." "I look forward to it. Au revoir, and be assured we will do everything possible to get your granddaughter back safely." "Au revoir Dominique, and thank you."

Rutherford called his secretary, "Call Georgina please, tell her I am going to France and ask if is she going to come with me. Get me a first-class flight to Charles de Gaulle airport as soon as possible and ring my butler and tell him to pack for me. I will probably require four or five days of clothes. I would like to leave this evening if possible. I may well have to stay in Paris overnight, so book me into the George V. I'll move on to stay as near as possible to Stephanie in Chamonix, so find a suitable hotel and if possible, get a suite. If Georgina is coming, please also sort out her travel arrangements. She'll probably need more time to pack than me, so might need to travel separately. Oh, and organise a car and chauffeur to collect me at the airport and to ferry me around," "Right away Mr Buchanan."

De Villepin called his secretary. "Get me a Capitaine Cadieux of the Police Nationale as soon as possible," Shortly afterwards his telephone rang. "Capitaine Cadieux Minister," and the secretary connected the call. Cadieux had never spoken to such a high-ranking minister before and was suitably nervous. "Cadieux, what is the progress on finding the child and the kidnappers," Cadieux nervously replied, "Sir, we have not yet received any ransom demand, so we are not certain that it is a kidnapping, although that is our main theory. Interpol, airports and ports are all looking for the car and occupants. All police forces, ports and airports in Europe have been placed on alert and we are searching within a 50 km radius of Annecy where they were last seen, apparently behaving like a normal happy family, The nanny and chauffeur have excellent references and would be unlikely kidnappers, but we are not ruling them out. It is as if the car and occupants have completely disappeared. It is possible that the car and all three passengers have been abducted by outside parties, but again there is no evidence of that, neither is there evidence that the chauffeur and nanny are complicit in a kidnap. My team are working 18 hours a day trying to find anything, anything that might give us a lead," "I have had the child's grandfather on the phone to me. He is very influential in America and has offered the help of the American Embassy should you require it. All I have to do is make the call," "Sir, I truly believe that we are doing everything possible to locate them, but of course if you think that the Americans may be able to help, I am happy to accept it. It is of paramount importance of that the child is found safe and well," "I'll call the Ambassador and set up a meeting with you, and in the meantime can you send me a full report of your enquiries to date?" "Of course, sir, I'll arrange that immediately. "

Chapter 22

Daniel and Lizzie drove back into Annecy where he bought two pay-as-you-go Nokia 8210 mobiles but needed to use one of the new Nokia chargers to charge up Izzy's phone. He used one of the new pay-as-you-go phones to login to his bank accounts and transferred £1000 from his savings account into his current account. They drove on to Lyon where with the rate of exchange being 0.7 euros to the pound, he withdrew €1400 cash in euros at an ATM and gave Lizzie €700 of the cash for her shopping expenses. They drove to Gare de la Part-Duex in the East of the city where Daniel, taking the Razr and one of the pay-as-you-go phones, boarded the 14.10 TGV train to Marseilles.

Lizzie and Klara, found a nice spot on the banks of The Saône and sitting in the warm spring sunshine enjoyed a pleasant lunch of the bread, patè, ham and cheese, followed by the crème caramel. Lizzie had a small bottle of beer and Klara, a carton of orange juice. After lunch Lizzie found a hypermarket, stocked up on groceries and bought some toys, games and children's books for Klara, then drove out of Lyon and on towards Valence, found an Aire on the A7, pulled in and made supper while Klara played with some of the toys.

Chapter 23

Cadieux was just getting out of his car when his mobile rang and he saw a withheld number. "Capitaine Cadieux speaking," "Good afternoon Capitaine, please hold for Ambassador Leach," and after a few seconds "Capitaine Cadieux, my name is Howard Leach, the

American Ambassador to France and I understand you have a problem with a missing child," Cadieux decided that to refuse any help from the Ambassador would not do his career prospects any good, so he said "Yes sir, I have, and I am most grateful for your call. I believe that we are doing everything possible to locate Miss Meier, but if you feel there is any help that you could provide, I would be very happy to receive it." "Would you be so kind as to forward me a full report on your enquiries to date and I will have my staff see what assistance we may be able to offer." "Of course, Ambassador it will be my pleasure." "Thank you Capitaine, can you think of anything I can do for you in the meantime which may be of help?" "I'm sorry sir, I cannot, but I welcome your assistance. " "I look forward to receiving your report and I wish you good luck in finding the child, goodbye." "Goodbye Mr. Ambassador." And the Ambassador ended the call. Phew he thought, the Interior Minister and the American Ambassador all in the space of half an hour. Cadieux breathed a huge sigh of relief and entered police H.Q. Cadieux called Laurent. "Pierre, I need to send a complete report of our enquiries to the American Ambassador in Paris, and also send copies to the Director General and the Interior Minister. Can you take Fournier and LeFevre off their current duties and compile the report as soon as possible? I know that we are doing everything possible, but we also have to be seen to be doing everything possible." "Yes sir, right away." "I'm going to the chalet; I'll be back in the office in an hour."

Chapter 24

Daniel arrived in Marseilles shortly after 5.30 and taking a bus out of the city centre, set his plan into action. Powering up the Razr, he inserted the SIM card, checked the caller list and saw that Marcus was the main caller. He linked his camera to the Razr, transferred a picture of Klara building the snowman, sent his first text message with the picture attached, switched off the Razr, removed the SIM, then got the next bus back to the St Charles railway station, bought a ticket to Paris and boarded the last train just before 8 pm, due to arrive at Paris Gare du Lyon around midnight. The mobile phone on the table in Chamonix buzzed with a message alert. Marcus opened his phone and read the text with a photo attachment of Klara playing in the snow building a snowman.

Klara is safe and well. Please do not involve the gendarme. That is unnecessary. Do not worry, no harm will come to her. Please wait for further instructions.

Stephanie and Capitaine Cadieux both looked at the message and the photo. "The message came from Alex. I just can't believe he would do such a thing," said Marcus, "and, to involve Izzy as well, is unforgivable." "Thank God she's okay, and she seems happy," Stephanie was weeping with joy at the text.

Capitaine Cadieux immediately got on his phone to headquarters. "We have received a text from Alex's phone. Have you traced the message?" "Not yet sir, but it shouldn't be long. The phone providers are monitoring all calls, although texts take a little longer apparently. I will call you as soon as it comes through." Cadieux said to Marcus "We must do nothing to alarm him. Play along with whatever he asks for, and see if we can catch him," "But we MUST prioritise getting Klara back safely," maintained Marcus. "Of course sir, that is our number one aim. I assure you that we will do nothing to endanger your daughter's life. Send a text back asking him to call you," So, Marcus did. "Alex, thank you for the photograph, but please call me. Why are you doing this? I'm sure we can sort this out between us. I thought you were happy working for us. There was no need for this. Where are you? I'll come and collect Klara, wherever you are. No questions asked," Marcus did not receive a reply. "I will arrange for more officers to come here and set up recording of any phone calls you might receive, although at present they seem to be relying on texts."

Cadieux spoke to Police HQ. "Alex has been in touch, calling Monsieur Meier's mobile phone. Send a team with telephone surveillance equipment to the chalet at once, and arrange a shift system for the monitoring of calls," Capitaine Cadieux's phone rang. "He's in Marseilles sir," reported H.Q., in a run-down area just outside the city centre." "Alert the Marseilles police department and ask for observations for the car and all three persons. Do not approach or allow them to know they are under observation, and contact me immediately they are found," "Very good sir." "And ask if they have CCTV in that area." Marseilles police assembled a team of plain clothes police, issued the photographs of Alex, Izzy, Klara and the Mercedes limousine, and sent them into the seedy area of Marseilles searching for the kidnappers.

Meanwhile, Daniel was enjoying a sandwich and a beer on the TGV as it headed northwards.

After supper, Lizzie read a book to Klara who was sitting on her knee, cuddling in tightly. Although the books were in French, Lizzie was enjoying trying to read them to Klara, even though her French pronunciation was dreadful and she didn't understand a word, but Klara seemed to be enjoying them, even if she didn't fully understand them either. She then put Klara to bed in the bunk bed in the pop-up roof, which she thought was a great adventure, and read her another story until Klara fell asleep. Now that she was alone, Lizzie began to worry. She loved looking after Klara but although Klara did not seem to be upset, the thought of her missing her parents was distressing her. Possibly it was because she was used to having nannies look after her. Would this insane scheme work? How confident was she that Daniel had worked out a fool proof plan? It seemed an excellent plan, but was she looking through rose-tinted glasses? Would she end up like her brother in prison. Would they end up being rich. Her mind was in a turmoil. She was giving herself a headache. She undressed and got ready for bed and settled down, but unfortunately sleep didn't come easily. She tossed and turned before falling into a fitful sleep. She dreamt she was in prison dressed in a trouser suit with arrows on it, her head had been shaved and everywhere she went, large barred doors kept closing in front of her making her go down dark passages wading through knee deep filthy water. It was dimly lit and the walls were slimy when she touched them. Cell doors on both sides of the passages opened and screaming harridans yelled obscenities at her from their cells. "Child stealer! Paedophile!" She woke in a cold sweat and looked at her watch. It was only half past eleven, she could not believe she had only been asleep for an hour. She got up, made herself a cup of tea, took a couple of paracetamol and eventually went back to sleep, and fortunately, this time, did not dream at all.

Chapter 25

Rutherford Wallace Buchanan-Hunt III arrived at Charles de Gaulle airport on the overnight Air France flight from JFK airport landing at 06.05. The seven-and-a-half-hour flight had been uneventful, and travelling first class, he had dined on scallops in a white wine sauce, fillet mignon rare, with a very nice 2019 Chateau Mouton Rothschild Premier Cru Classe Pauillac, to wash it down followed by a creme brulé and coffee. As he had expected, his wife Georgina needed more time to pack, and was flying to Paris on the same flight a day later. "I recommend the scallops and filet mignon," he told her after he landed. The Air Bus A350 flight wasn't quite as quick as he was used to, regularly travelling on Concorde to both London and Paris, often discussing world affairs with Dr Henry Kissinger or Sir David Frost, but since the dreadful fatal crash of the Air France Concorde in July 2000 which resulted in the loss of 113 lives, Concorde had eventually been retired from service, much to the chagrin of its regular customers and the thousands of dreamers who hoped one day to be able to afford the air fare. He had managed to get almost three hours sleep and had been pleasantly surprised at the level of comfort on this new aircraft, much more room than on Concorde, if not quite as fast.

On clearing customs and immigration, he phoned Stephanie. "Hi darling, I've just landed in Paris and I have appointments to see the Interior Minister and the American Ambassador today. I'm staying in the George V in Paris tonight and then I'm coming to Chamonix with your mother when she arrives tomorrow morning," "Daddy thank you for coming, we are both terribly worried and it will be lovely to see you both. We had a photo and a text last night from Alex saying not to worry, she won't be harmed but not to involve the Gendarme, which is a little bit late as they already are. I don't see how we can cancel them. I cannot believe that of Alex, I hope he hasn't hurt Izzy, or maybe Izzy is infatuated and doing it with him. I just don't know what to believe," "Try not to worry too much darling, I'll speak to the Interior Minister and the Ambassador later today and see what help they can be, but the text seems to be positive news that she won't be harmed. Try to stay positive and I'll let you know if I can get some additional help," "OK Daddy, we'll see you tomorrow. Bye for now," "Bye darling,"

He left arrivals and saw a uniformed man wearing a cap holding a card with 'Mr Buchanan-Hunt' in large writing on it. He introduced himself and the chauffeur picked up Rutherford's case. "Let me take that for you sir," And took him outside to a gleaming limousine. Rutherford got into the rear and settled back into the leather upholstery, and closed his eyes for several minutes. They headed straight to the office of the Interior Minister where he was shown in immediately and warmly embraced with la bise (a kiss on both cheeks) as is the French custom. "Coffee, or something stronger, Rutherford?" The minister enquired. "Coffee would be fine Dominique, thank you. I am still somewhat tired after the flight, although the flight was comfortable and I did sleep a little. It is good to see you again Dominique, but perhaps under different circumstances it would be more pleasant," Dominique asked his secretary to organise coffee, and then "I agree Rutherford, but better than not meeting at all. What is the latest news on your granddaughter, Klara isn't it?" "Yes, it is Klara, and she is just two and a half. Her parents are worried sick as you can imagine," "Yes, I also have grandchildren and love to spend as much time with them as my schedule permits. We have a villa on the Camargue and I try to get there with the family every few weeks. You and your family must join us when this dreadful business is over," "That would be delightful, thank you," Coffee arrived and while they sat Dominique said "I have spoken to the Director General and Capitaine Cadieux and he has sent me the fully detailed report as to the extent of his enquiries. I must say he seems to have done everything I would have expected." "I heard from Stephanie this morning that the chauffeur has sent a text saying Klara will not be harmed, but not to involve the Gendarme. Is there anything else you can do, involve any other department, or draft in other resources," "Not really Rutherford, although that is good news regarding the text. The Police Departments are working together doing everything they can, so there is no lack of resources. I know this is a difficult and frightening situation, and I would love to tell you that there is something else I could do, but believe me, our officers are doing everything possible to locate your granddaughter," "Thank you Dominique, I am not doubting the capabilities of your police officers, but it is obviously a most distressing situation and my daughter and son-in-law are desperately worried. I am going to see the American Ambassador this afternoon to see if he can offer any assistance," "A good idea Rutherford, I am happy to pass on any information they require," "I hope we can meet again soon in very different circumstances. Au Revoir my friend,"

Chapter 26

The incident room at police HQ had filled up from 6 am with all detectives compiling their reports for the morning briefing at 7. At five minutes to 7, Cadieux marched into the room with his mobile phone pressed to his ear, talking rapidly. He listened for quite a while and then a brusque "Sir" as he hung up. "What have we found out ladies and gentlemen? the Director General is now personally looking at the case and I need to keep him updated. The Interior Minister is breathing down his neck, which means the Director General is breathing down my neck which means .... ?" Fournier again "You are breathing down our necks sir." "Correct Fournier, so what have we found out, Eh?" Silence greeted his question. "Nothing? Nothing at all?" "Sorry sir," It was Laurent who spoke up being the senior amongst the detectives. "There is no trace at all. The Marseilles police searched the area, but could not find the car or the occupants. They carried out a door-to-door search, but as it is a well-known area for drugs and prostitution, the response was predictably disappointing." "Heard nothing, saw nothing Eh?" "That's right sir. The mobile company report that his mobile is now switched off and there has been no further contact." "Very well, Mm... very disappointing. What about CCTV," "There are no CCTV cameras at all in that area of Marseilles sir. Apparently, it is in the budget for some to be installed next year, but nothing yet. The railway station does have a few cameras, but the station was very busy. No sign of a small child other than a baby in a push chair," "But why has there been no ransom demand? It doesn't make sense, and we also now have the added pressure of the Director General and the Interior Minister on our backs. Apparently, the girls grandfather knew the Minister personally so has called in a favour. Anything else?" "Yes sir," it was Girard, "The mobile companies have sent through the transcripts of the recent texts on both Alex and Izzy's phones. Alex appears to be a bit of a ladies man, especially with the nannies. There are several texts to and from the previous nannies expressing romantic feelings, and then the nannies leave and he moves on to the next one without compunction, probably enjoying his bachelorhood. The texts to Izzy are still of a friendly nature rather than romantic. Nothing in the texts relate to a potential kidnap. Izzy on the other hand has been much more suggestive in her texts to Alex, and also to two of her friends where she says she is crazy about him and hopes he will feel the same. Obviously, a smitten teenager. Again though, nothing suggesting a kidnap plan." "Right, Erm... have you checked if any of the previous nannies got pregnant with Alex? Could maybe provide a motive for revenge perhaps. What about the texts received from each of their phones? How does that all tie in?" "It just doesn't make sense at all sir," replied Poirier. "We must think outside of the box, what are we missing, and while we are missing out, the trail is growing colder. Ok think about this and see if you can come up with an answer. And the sooner the better."

Chapter 27

Daniel had stayed in a small hotel very near to the Gare du Lyon, checking in after midnight. He did not check out, but sat at a small café having a croissant and coffee for breakfast. He called Lizzie. "How are you and Klara, Everything OK?" "Yes, yes, she's fine, playing with the toys and I read a book to her last night in my new second language. I did have an awful nightmare last night, but I will tell you about it when I see you. We are just about to go shopping for some new clothes for her," "Take a picture of Klara on Izzy's phone, with something showing date and time clearly. Send it to Marcus. Then switch off, remove the SIM and move away from there straight away. I have been busy buying more 'off the peg' companies online in Belize, Hong Kong, Panama and the Seychelles, and I've opened offshore bank accounts for each of them using both mine and your documents and shared the companies between us. I've spread the bank accounts across several countries

95

to try to disguise any transactions. I will close down some of the companies and their bank accounts as soon as possible when they have served their purpose. I'm going to hire a car later and then I'll come down and meet up. Text me your location when you stop for the night but keep moving to new locations and I'll see you later, I think it's all going to plan." "I'm just outside Saint Rambert d'Albon and I'll try to buy Klara some clothes there, then drive back to Lyon to send the text," "Brilliant, try to keep a watch for CCTV anywhere, just in case. Love you, Bye" "I Love you too, be careful."

Lizzie, surreptitiously looking out for any CCTV, but trying not to appear suspicious found a small children's clothes shop, took Klara in and bought her a new outfit of warm clothing and changes of underwear using the cash Daniel had given her. Returning to the camper she dressed Klara in the new clothes, bought a copy of La Monde, and with Klara holding the paper showing the headline took a photo. She drove into Lyon, sent it to Marcus, with the caption *Klara reading Le Monde* then turned round and drove towards Bourg-en-Bresse. When she arrived at Bourg-en-Bresse, she found an Aire on the A40 and sent a text to Daniel with her location.

At 11.55 the notification sound on his mobile alerted Marcus. He opened the photograph of Klara, smiling holding Le Monde showing the headline clearly. There was no message only the caption. He showed the picture to Stephanie who said "That's marvellous, and she is smiling, but they aren't her clothes. Her own coat isn't blue, it's green," "The picture came from Izzy's phone, so they must be working together. I'll send it on to Cadieux, and then I'm going to call Hunter-Smythe." "Don't you think you should leave that to the police? You don't want to interfere with their enquiries." "Yes, I know, you're right, I'm just so angry that they have deceived us." He forwarded the picture pointing out that the hat and coat were different to what she was wearing when she had been taken.

Cadieux circulated the latest picture to the assembled detectives and asked "Okay, we now have a text from Izzy's phone, so it looks like they must be working together. Do we know where the photograph was sent from," It was Girard who was tracking all calls who replied "Not yet sir, I'll get onto it right away." "The girls clothes have changed. As soon as we find out where the text was from, I want children's clothes shops in the area checked and if possible, CCTV in the shops looked at." Cadieux went through to the telephone call centre they had set up following the reward offer by Marcus. "Has anyone had anything useful from the calls?" All of the officers answering the phones shook their heads with mutterings of "No sir." "It's actually been very quiet sir," said the senior gendarme. "A couple of crank calls, one saying they saw her picked up by a spaceship, and about half a dozen genuine calls with possible sightings which have been sent out immediately to the Police Municipale for checking, but so far nothing positive," "Thank you," and Cadieux returned to the incident room.

Daniel searched the internet for a car hire close to the station, and found one only four streets away. He chose a small non-descript grey Citroen Saxa and drove into the long stay car park at Orly airport. He sat for some time waiting until he saw a similar Citroen pull into the car park. The driver unloaded two large suitcases and waited for the shuttle bus to take him to the terminal. He waited for 10 minutes and then carefully looking for CCTV cameras and that no one was looking he swapped the number plates on the two cars. He then drove out of the airport and found an Aire on the A6 Autoroute, pulled in behind a large articulated lorry, disconnected the speedometer and continued on towards Lyon. As he was approaching Macon he saw a text from Lizzie, so he altered his route to Bourg-en-Bresse and the Aire on the A40.

Chapter 28

Francoise Desjardins was sitting at the dining table in a small detached cottage eating his breakfast when his pal, Gabriel Lavigne, knocked at the front door. His mother let him in, dusting flour from her hands and wiping them on her apron "Come in Gabriel, he's just finishing his breakfast, he won't be long. I'm baking today so there'll be cake for you this afternoon. Would you like anything" "No thank you Madame Desjardins, I'll just wait for Francoise." The fourteen-year-olds had been inseparable since they became friends at primary school. The house was neat and tidy and had a small garden to both the front and rear. The was a wood burning stove in the kitchen making the room nice and warm and there was always a large pot of something tasty simmering on the stove. Monsieur Desjardins was very proud of the way he tended his vegetable patch which had provided a good supply of seasonal vegetables throughout the year. There was a small chicken run which housed six chickens and eggs were mostly quite plentiful. Madame Desjardins looked after the flower garden to the front of the house and she always managed to have a display of something in a vase on the kitchen table. She was a jolly person, slightly overweight and with a ruddy complexion from working in her garden. She was always singing around the house and had a ready laugh. Francoise finished his breakfast and leapt up to greet his pal. "Not before you've cleared up" his mother scolded. Gabriel helped his friend clear the breakfast things away, then went outside. Francoise mother shouted after them "Don't forget your sandwiches and drinks boys." They went back inside and filled their backpacks with the sandwiches, drinks and cakes left out for them.

The boys were looking forward to getting their toboggans out again and spending Sunday playing on the snow in the hills outside Thones. They had enjoyed tobogganing all day on Saturday, but the slopes had been a bit tame for the two daredevils. Both wrapped up in warm clothing with scarves, gloves and woolly hats, they set off pulling their toboggans behind them, and headed for the best slopes they could find. They had looked out of their school windows at the snow falling during the week, and hoped it would be clear for some serious fun at the weekend. It was a fine morning, and like yesterday, the sun was shining from a clear blue sky. A slight thaw had set in as they walked along the road heading out of the village towards Chamonix where they knew of a ravine where the slopes were quite steep, and it looked like it would be another good day today.

Finding their spot, they climbed over the roadside barriers and nervously looked down into the ravine. "That looks very steep Francoise." "You're not chicken Gabriel, are you?" "'Course not" he replied but they did set off on some of the gentler slopes first, climbing back up the slopes for another run and gaining confidence they gradually chose steeper and longer routes. The snow was still quite soft, and they were having a good time. They picked another route to try, steep at first plateauing a little, then steep again down to the bottom of the ravine. The longest one yet, and the steepest. It looked a long way. "You first Gabriel, then I'll pass you," boasted Francoise. Gabriel going first, picked up speed, levelled out on the plateau, then over the ridge and speeding up down the second slope. Almost at the bottom he saw what appeared to be a rock just ahead of him. He managed to swerve past the rock, but in doing so fell off the toboggan and crashed into a snowdrift. A huge snowfall engulfed him, but fortunately Francoise was following him, and pulled him out of the pile of snow. They were both convulsed with laughter at Gabriel's misfortune, but when they stopped laughing, they saw that the snowfall had uncovered some shiny black metal. They scraped more snow away and saw more black metal and a door handle. "Gabriel, I think there's a car here," exclaimed Francoise.

Chapter 29

Rutherford left the office of the Interior Minister, starting to feel the effects of jet lag kicking in, so he asked the chauffeur to find a suitable place for lunch. The driver knew of a small bistro close by, so Rutherford enjoyed a light lunch after which he was driven to the American Embassy on the Avenue Gabriel, just off the Place de la Concorde. The Embassy is the oldest diplomatic mission of the United States established by its first Ambassador, Benjamin Franklin in 1779, and some of the other Founding Fathers, were the earliest United States Ambassadors to France. Arriving well before his scheduled appointment, he waited in an ante-room with a pot of coffee on the side table until he was shown into the Ambassador's office which was decorated with several paintings of previous ambassadors. Howard Leach rose from behind his desk to greet him. "Mr Buchanan-Hunt, I'm very pleased to meet you," "Rutherford please Mr Ambassador. Thank you for seeing me," "I hope I am able to be of assistance Rutherford. This is obviously a very trying time for you and your family. I have read the reports from the French police and the officer in charge, Capitaine Cadieux, appears very thorough, however I have assigned one of my attaché's to look into the kidnap. Obviously, we are restricted as to what we are permitted to do on foreign soil, but we have access to other sources of information that may prove helpful." The Ambassador called his secretary "Can you ask Philip to join us." A few minutes later a very tall, well over 6 feet, young man in naval uniform entered the office. The Ambassador introduced him. "Philip, this is Mr Buchanan-Hill, grandfather of the missing little girl, Rutherford, this is my Naval attaché, Lieutenant Philip Constantine, who has been reviewing the case on my behalf, and has my full confidence but I am afraid I must leave you as I have an engagement at the Elyseè Palace. Please make yourselves comfortable here and if there is anything you need, or coffee, tea, just ask my secretary. Rutherford, it was a pleasure meeting you and I hope we can help finding your granddaughter." With that the Ambassador left the room leaving Rutherford and Philip to review the case.

"What have you been able to find out Philip, have you heard about the text that was received last night?" Asked Rutherford. "Well sir, yes I heard from Capitaine Cadieux this morning that the chauffer had sent a text with a picture of Klara, but other than that not a lot I'm afraid. Firstly, I can tell you that this Capitaine Cadieux is a very experienced officer and has successfully secured the release of three kidnap victims. He has assembled a large team and is following up several lines of enquiry. He has sent a detailed report on his enquiries to date and it is a most unusual case and is not following a normal kidnapping pattern, if there is such a thing. I have spoken to our military and asked them if they can review any footage they have of the area and our technical department is also investigating all communications. I have asked for this to be top priority and will keep you informed of any progress." "That is comforting to know, thank you for your efforts, Philip." "Can you think of anything else I can help you with Mr Buchannan?" "I can't think of anything, but then I haven't had anyone kidnapped before." They left the Ambassador's office, Philip returning to his own office and Rutherford to his limousine to take him to the George V hotel in the 8th arrondissement.

Chapter 30

Daniel was trying to think of a way he could convince her parents that Klara was safe and well. He stopped at an Aire on the A6 and asked Lizzie who said "Can't you look on the internet and find out the nursery rhyme she says, something about daumen." "What a good idea." He searched Google and found the nursery rhyme, which also had the English translation about the thumb which shakes the plum. He copied it to his phone, then switched on the Razr copied the poem into a text, took a deep breath and sent another text to Marcus

Klara will be handed back to you safe and well in exchange for $400,000 US dollars in unmarked used $50 notes. Not a lot for your lovely daughter. NO GENDARME UNDER ANY CIRCUMSTANCES. Further instructions will follow. Text your reply YES, I WILL COMPLY.

Klara says

"Das ist der Daumen
der schüttelt die Pflaumen,
der hebt sie auf,
der trägt sie nach Haus,
und der Kliene isst sie alle auf,"
You have 1 hour.

And then switched off the Razr.

Marcus sat with Stephanie and read and reread the message. Stephanie said "That is the nursery rhyme that Izzy and I taught Klara," They could see Officer Benoit was looking at them from time to time, so had a whispered conversation and agreed not to tell the Capitaine of the demand. Marcus and Stephanie hugged each other. "I'm sure they don't mean to harm her," Stephanie was also trying to be positive "They wouldn't have sent her picture otherwise, and they have bought new clothes for her. She looked happy as well," Benoit called Cadieux and said "Sir, I think the kidnappers have made contact. Marcus and Stephanie have been looking at text messages frequently and talking in whispers," "Well done, Benoit, I'm on my way. Girard, contact the mobile operators, it maybe that a text has been sent and I want to know what it says, if they won't tell me" "Right away sir." Cadieux left for the chalet.

Chapter 31

Arriving at the chalet he confronted Marcus and Stephanie "Any news, anything you want to tell me?" Cadieux noticed a quick glance between the two. There was a long silence, then he said "You have had a message haven't you," "We can't tell you," "Please let me help you. If you won't tell me, I can't help you." Stephanie was obviously distressed and quietly said "We can't, you must understand. No gendarme under any circumstances. We cannot put Klara in danger." Cadieux was silent for a few moments the said "Okay, well, technically we are not the Gendarme, we are the Police Nationale," "I think you are splitting hairs Capitaine" responded Marcus. Cadieux thought for a moment, stroking his chin, then "Okay, I understand your concerns. Let me make you an offer. Let me see the message and advise you and I promise I will not instigate any action without your approval," Marcus and Stephanie looked at each other, "What do you think," said Marcus. "I don't trust the police; they haven't done anything," replied Stephanie. "I just want Klara home; we can afford the money easily. I am just surprised it isn't more," "Stephanie, I think that's being a little unfair on the Capitaine and his men, they are trying very hard to find Klara, and it isn't them that have taken her." "Please, let me see the message, not as a policeman but hopefully, as a friend," They looked at each other, uncertainty etched on their haggard faces, then Stephanie nodded. "Show him" she said.

Marcus showed Cadieux the text, and he studied it. After several moments he said "This is most unusual, yes most unusual, on two counts. First, the sum is, well a strange amount. Why $400,000 and not half a million. Most kidnappers would round it up to that amount at least, a million even. You are known to be very wealthy, and from a very wealthy family, and second, there is no threat if you do not pay. Kidnappers usually threaten something nasty if you do not pay, but there is a complete absence of threat. I do not understand it at all," "I'm sure neither Alex or Izzy would hurt Klara, so the absence of a threat to harm her does not surprise me," Stephanie said. "I am as confused as you, what do you suggest we do, Capitaine," said Marcus. Stephanie then decided it was time to put her foot down. Glaring at Marcus she screamed "What do you suggest we do Capitaine, what is the matter with you? I thought we had agreed we would pay the ransom. If you won't pay, then I will. I will call Daddy and arrange the payment from my trust fund. I will not let anything prevent my daughter from being safe. And the police can go and rot in hell," and threw herself sobbing onto the couch. "Of course, we will pay the money Darling, we agreed that," said Marcus, going to her side and putting his arm around her held her tight, comforting her, "I want her back just as much as you do, and then once she is safely back with us, the Capitaine will try to apprehend Alex and Izzy, I was only asking Cadieux for his suggestion. They won't get far, will they Cadieux?" "No Marcus, I can assure you that we will be hot on their trail. They will have nowhere to hide." "I will send the text message back to them," Turning to Cadieux "I must have your assurance that you will do nothing to hamper the handover of the ransom. I will assist you in every way after we get Klara back but until then I will follow the instructions to the letter, and I want no interference," "Of course, you have my word, with the proviso that you keep in touch with me," So Marcus agreed and sent the text, *I will comply. Please let me see Klara again.* And Cadieux drove back to Police H.Q.

Arriving back in the incident room, "Sir," it was Bertrand, "The text was from Izzy, she was in the Lyon area," "Right, contact the Lyon Police Municipale, Gendarmerie and Nationale, check the shops as soon as possible. Now, they may be together, or, they took a train back from Marseilles," He mused, again stroking his chin, something that had become a habit when reflecting on information. "Contact the railway station and find out if they got off a train last night in Lyon," "Yes sir," Maybe, Cadieux thought, just maybe, we have a breakthrough.

When Daniel received the text, he could hardly believe his eyes. Don't get carried away he said to himself. This is only the first step, getting agreement. Not only do we have to get the money, but also not get caught afterwards. That could be tricky. He was aware that despite his message not to involve the police, the police were looking for Klara and there would be no guarantee they would not try to hunt them down. His plan has to be fool proof. Time to put the next part into action, but first he called Lizzie. "Take another photo of Klara, send it, and move immediately,"

Lizzie took Klara to a park and stood her beside a large bush so that her location could not be identified. She put the SIM card into the mobile phone, switched it on, took a picture with Klara, sent it off with the caption *Klara in the park*, switched off the phone and removed the SIM. The phone was switched on for no more than three minutes. Lizzie walked back from the park, she and Klara got back into the camper and drove out of the town towards Bourg-on-Bresse. Daniel sent another text to Marcus
You have your proof that Klara is well. Klara is looking forward to be with her mummy and daddy again. Send a text when you have the money available.

Marcus saw the photo and showed it to Stephanie, but said "she looks well, but there's no proof that it was taken today," Marcus had contacted his bank immediately following the ransom demand and had arranged for the money to be sent to him by special courier. He made sure that they understood the need to have the money as soon as possible, and that it was in unmarked used notes. It arrived at 20 past four and Marcus sent a text confirming its arrival. He telephoned his Bank Manager. "Monsieur Meier, I hope the money has arrived safely." "Yes about 10 minutes ago, please

confirm that the notes are unmarked and numbers unrecorded."
"Yes sir, exactly as your instructions. We realise the delicate nature
of this transaction."

Every half hour Daniel had checked his texts, then switched off the
phone and kept moving, not always in the same direction. He saw
the reply from Marcus at 4.30. The money was available much
earlier than he had anticipated. He phoned Lizzie "We are on, get
ready to deliver Klara as soon as the money has cleared," Daniel
sent another text
*Be ready to drive tomorrow morning. You will then receive further
instructions.*

Cadieux felt he needed a break, so he walked outside in the spring
air, still thinking about the case. He walked along Rue la Mollard
and turned left into the open space and wandered up towards the
edge of the trees. He always felt at peace and calm when walking
amongst the trees. He considered all of the information he had, but
still struggled to make sense of it all. After half an hour he returned
to the incident room and saw that most of the desks were empty,
but Girard was still at his, working on his computer. "What about
Lyon?" he asked "The Municipale and Gendarme have scoured the
area, a good number of clothes shops have already been visited but
none sold a blue coat for a two to three-year-old. More shops are
being visited today. Some shops have CCTV but as they hadn't sold
the coat the footage has not been checked, although they have
been asked to send a copy to us here," "Yes, good, what about the
railway station?" "Again sir, there were no sightings of either the
couple or the little girl and they do not appear to have boarded or
got off a train," "Right thank you, they are obviously very mobile so
we should not rule anything out. Have Interpol come back with
anything?" "No sir. Nothing at all. And all ports and airports have
reported in with no passengers matching their description," "Well

that just leaves us with cars, oh and I suppose buses. They may have switched cars of course, which does make things quite difficult.

Chapter 32

Cadieux was sitting at his desk going over his detectives reports when a uniformed officer knocked and entered. "Sir, there has been a development," "Yes, what is it," "Two 14-year-old boys, Francoise Desjardins and Gabriel Lavigne have found a car in a snow drift between Annecy and Chamonix. The plates are the same as the missing Mercedes and inside were the bodies of a man in his twenties or thirties, and a girl about twenty with blond hair. They appear to be Aleksander and Isabella. The car had crashed down a hillside and had been covered with snow until the boys who were out tobogganing, found it this morning. The local Gendarme are sending pictures over for verification," "Any sign of the child?" "No sir, the child seat was unbuckled and empty," "Have the boys been interviewed?" "Yes sir, initially the Traffic Officers interviewed them and took their details for a statement to be taken by your officers." So, mused Cadieux if that is Alex and Izzy, who has Klara. "Have the forensic team been called," "Yes sir, they are already at the scene," "Give me the location and I will go there immediately. Circulate this information to all of the teams please and make sure there is a news blackout until I have informed the parents," "Yes sir,"

On arriving at the scene, the traffic officers of the Gendarmerie had called the police doctor, who had confirmed the deaths of the two occupants. As soon as it was realised that this was the subject of the potential kidnapping, Capitaine Cadieux had been informed and the bodies were not to be removed until he arrived and released them from the scene. The area around the car was cordoned off as a possible crime scene and, as per normal practice, the forensic team had been called. The forensic team dressed in white overalls, boots, face masks and head coverings were almost invisible from view from the road above. They were meticulously placing items in polythene bags whilst a crime scene officer was recording every item saved. A photographer was taking pictures from every angle. Cadieux stood at the side of the road looking down on the crash site. The road had been completely closed to all traffic, with diversions set up. As the senior officer investigating the missing persons, now believed to be a kidnap, it was his decision regarding all matters including removals of bodies and the car.

As he surveyed the scene, a traffic officer approached him. "Lieutenant Devereaux sir, we have seen signs of a collision on the cliff face about 200 meters away. The forensic team are taking paint and glass samples, but I believe it was where the Mercedes struck the cliff on the wrong side of the road and then crossed the road and over the edge into the ravine," "Thank you Lieutenant, please show me." Cadieux walked along the road and examined the marks and agreed with the traffic officer. "Yes, this does look like the car struck the cliff face here. I wonder why it was on the wrong side of the road. Alex was a very competent driver. Most unusual,"

Cadieux returned to the edge of the ravine and looked down on the crash site again. A tent had been erected over the car affording some protection from the weather and as darkness was falling, a generator was chugging away powering lights illuminating the scene. Ropes had been secured forming a safe route down to the car and very gingerly he made his way down to the car holding on tightly to the makeshift rope handrail. He donned the protective overalls, boots, gloves and mask, entered the tent, saw the Mercedes impaled on a tree and looking into the car saw the bodies of what appeared to be Alex and Izzy. Both were wearing seat belts. He spoke to the police doctor. "Good afternoon doctor, what are you able to tell me," "Well Capitaine, nothing definitive at present, except that they both died several days ago, a more detailed time of death I can confirm after a post-mortem examination. Neither body appears at first inspection, to have injuries other than what I would expect from such an horrific car crash from the road down to here and being impaled on the tree. Again, to be confirmed after the PM," "The last confirmed sighting we have of the car and its occupants was in Annecy on Tuesday the 22nd around 2.45 p.m. if that's any help." "Thanks, Capitaine, it gives me a starting point." "What about the missing child," "The child car seat belt is uncoupled, not broken, appears in working condition and to have been released," "Could the child have been in the car at the time of the crash," "It is certainly possible, probably more likely than not, and I am sure your forensic officers will be able to confirm if that were the case," "Mmm…, thank you doctor, the bodies may be removed as soon as forensics say so, and please let me have the result of your post mortems as soon as possible," "Certainly Capitaine,"

Speaking to the tall senior forensic officer, Lieutenant Armand, who at 6 feet 4 inches towered over the diminutive Capitaine, Cadieux asked "When will you be able to remove the bodies and recover the car to the police yard?" "I think the bodies could be removed now as we have as much as we are going to be able to get here. The car will probably have to wait until tomorrow as darkness is going to be causing additional difficulties and we have to get a crane to lift it back up to the road. It is going to be quite tricky, with the steep slope covered in snow, and we don't want to lose any evidence. The car may even need to be wrapped, so it will take some time," "Have you been able to get any evidence from inside yet?" "Not much I'm afraid, again it is a question of not wanting to lose anything or contaminate it. We have carefully bagged the hands of the bodies and we will take great care in removing them. We may of course see something when the bodies are out of the car, but I think it unlikely," "Do you think that the child was in the car when it crashed?" "Well, there is a small patch of blood on the edge of the child's car seat. We will have it tested to see if it could belong to the child and it may have been there some time of course, but it does seem likely that the child was in the car, Yes" "OK Armand, thank you. Please let me know as soon as you have anything, however small," "Will do Capitaine,"

Chapter 33

Lizzie had moved on from Bourg-en-Bresse to the small village of Saint-Amour and found a parking place on the D912 next to the forest. She sent a text to Daniel with the location and just after seven Daniel pulled up alongside the camper. "Hi Klara," Daniel said giving her a hug, which she returned, before kissing Lizzie hello. Klara allowed herself to be picked up in his arms and he gave her a tight squeeze. Lizzie had a pasta meal ready for them, with another bottle of vin blanc, and he gratefully tucked in before relaxing on the settee. Lizzie put Klara to bed in the top bunk again, read her a story from the French book and when Klara was asleep, Daniel and Lizzie reviewed their progress. "In view of our last discussion, I thought that this place was rather appropriate." Daniel looked confused. "Saint-Amour? Saint of love. Don't you think that's what it means." Daniel laughed, "Quite probably, am I your Saint then." "Oh yes, definitely." Then more seriously he said "Tomorrow we have to be very careful. Despite my warnings to Marcus, I am sure the police will be looking for us, so we must give them no chance to find us, but don't worry, if we stick to the plan, it should, no, will, work perfectly. I'm going to drive over to Lyon tonight and stay at an Ibis and get prepared for the ransom drop. I'll keep in touch and let you know when to carry out your part of the plan." "Be careful darling." She replied, giving him huge hug and a long kiss. Eventually he left for Lyon.

Cadieux returned to the chalet and Marcus answered his knock on their door looking expectantly. "Good evening Marcus, I think we might have some hopefully positive, but strange news," Cadieux joined Marcus and Stephanie in the lounge. "What has happened?" Stephanie wanted to know. "Your car has been found on the road between Annecy and Chamonix. It was covered in snow in a snow drift but unfortunately there are two bodies inside. From the photographs you gave me they appear to be Alex and Izzy. Would you be able to confirm their identify?"

Cadieux showed them photographs of the car and Marcus confirmed that it was his car and the bodies were those of Alex and Izzy. "Are they dead," he asked. "I'm afraid so, and they seem to have been there for some time." "What about Klara?" Stephanie wailed. "The child seat was empty and you have had photographs showing Klara is alive and well. So, obviously they did not take Klara and the questions now appear to be, who has got her and what do they want? The car was covered in snow in the middle of a snow drift at the bottom of a ravine. Now please don't get alarmed, but there was a very small amount of blood on the child's car seat. Do you know about that?" "No" Stephanie sobbed. "Poor Klara is she alright," "Yes yes, I am sure if that was caused by the crash, it only suggests that Klara was in the car at the time of the accident. It is not major and nothing to worry about. Do you know if both Alex and Izzy definitely had their mobile phones with them?" "Alex always has his," replied Marcus "and I would expect that Izzy does as well," "Yes, she had," confirmed Stephanie. "This is now starting to make sense to me. As neither of the mobile phones are in the car, it would appear that someone must have taken Klara and the mobile phones from the car after the accident. You might not think it now, but Klara is a very lucky little girl. The car left the road on a sharp bend and is at the bottom of a very steep ravine some 300 metres down, as you can see from the photographs, the car is badly damaged. Both Alex and Izzy were wearing their seat belts, but that didn't prevent the massive injuries they sustained.

I think that because Klara was in the rear of the car, she did not suffer the same trauma as the front seat passengers did. She would not have been able to get away from the car on her own, probably wouldn't have been able to get out of the car even if she had been able to unbuckle her seat belt, so whilst it is not good that Klara has been taken, it is now 6 days since she disappeared, and without food, water and warmth, I think it is almost certain that she would also have died in the car if she had not been taken. The picture of Klara is obviously good news, and she is being well cared for. This is very positive and you must take comfort from that fact. At least she is alive, and we will find her. They obviously realise that the wellbeing of Klara is vital. We must wait now for the next message and their next move, although as we now have no leads on who may have her coupled with the fact that they are not using the Mercedes car, it does now complicate the issue. However, they are using the mobile phones of Alex and Izzy, which of course makes sense why they are using text messages. They wanted us to still think it was Alex and Izzy who had taken Klara, and you would not have recognised their voices in a phone call.

We have obviously put a trace on both of the phones, and the mobile providers are being very helpful in tracing the location of the text messages, although that does take time, and they are still being very mobile, switching off the phones and removing the SIM cards so it is very difficult to track them. The messages have been coming through from widely separated places, so we must assume that there are at least two persons involved, one using Alex's phone and one using Izzie's. This now appears to me to be not an organised abduction, but perhaps an opportunistic one. We don't yet know the cause of death of Alex and Izzy, but will know more after the post-mortems. We will need formal identification of the bodies at the morgue. This does not have to be done immediately, and I will arrange for you to be collected. The team will remain here in case of any phone calls and Officer Benoit will still stay with you and can get hold of me at any time," "I knew in my heart of hearts that Izzy could not have taken Klara away, or Alex for that matter," Stephanie maintained. "I am sorry I doubted them as well, but the texts from their phones made it look incriminating."

Marcus and Stephanie sat together on the sofa in the chalet lounge. Cadieux sitting opposite. Marcus was trying to be positive, although Stephanie was not coping well. "We have to be strong Steph; Klara is at least alive and safe and we have photos showing her looking happy. Whoever has her has obviously saved her life and for that we must be grateful. In fact, I'm overjoyed. I'm not too happy about them now trying to get more money from us, for goodness sake I've offered €50,000 as a reward and they're being greedy. We'll obviously pay the ransom, but I am very annoyed about it. After we get Klara back, I'll move heaven and earth to find them." "Marcus, I just want my little girl back safe and well, but I am also thinking of Alex and poor Izzy. She had her whole life ahead of her and was so looking forward to going up to university, studying law and following in her father's footsteps. Her parents will be devastated, she was an only child. Will the police tell them or is it something we should do? I promised her mother I would be in touch as soon as I heard anything." "I think the police will see to that, won't you Cadieux?" "We will ask the British police to speak to her parents, and they will probably want to come over to see Izzy," "Okay, thank you. I must say I wasn't looking forward to that conversation," "Stephanie, having done that three or four times, I can say it is the most unpleasant duty I've ever had to undertake.

All you need to do now is concentrate on helping us get Klara back safe and well," and Marcus, turning to Stephanie said "I wonder how the car ended up in the ravine. Alex is a very safe driver and I've never had the slightest concern about his driving. I know he is…er… was, very conscientious and took great care, especially with Klara in the car," "Is his father still alive?" "Yes, I believe so, I know his mother died several years ago, and I assume the police will also be arranging for him to be told, is that right Cadieux?" "Yes, we will also arrange that." "I didn't get the impression from Alex that he was particularly well off, so if he wishes to come here, I'm happy to pay his costs in getting here from Gdansk." "Could there have been an accident?" asked Stephanie "We are still investigating the cause, and at present there are no signs of another vehicle being involved, but we are still looking." "Why have they kept Klara all this time, what are they thinking about," "Who knows, it makes no sense at all. If you are right and it was not organised, presumably they are still working out what to do. Perhaps we should put out another appeal, directly to the kidnappers, maybe increase the reward, what do you think Cadieux?" "I think another appeal could be a good idea, but I wouldn't increase the reward. They have already issued a demand for $400,000 so increasing your reward isn't likely to interest them, unless you top that, which I think would be a mistake, and the reward is sufficient for a member of the public to contact us if they know anything. No, let us wait until tomorrow morning and if there are no developments, we will consider another televised appeal in the afternoon. But most of all remember, in all probability they have taken her from a crashed car in the middle of a snow drift, and saved her life, so they will not want to harm her, I must get back to HQ to co-ordinate the search of the area." "Bye Cadieux." He hurried back to his car, drove back to police H.Q.

Chapter 34

Sitting at his desk he went over his file again reading and re-reading it, trying to find anything they had missed. Nothing obvious leapt out. There was no real line of enquiry to follow. It was a breakthrough that the car had been found, but with Alex and Izzy being found dead, that complicated everything. Who had taken Klara? What did they want? Why had there been no ransom demand. Whilst he now believed this to be opportunistic, as much as he didn't wish to do so, was he going to have to wait until a ransom demand was made and hope that gave him some options or could the car have been forced off the road by a gang and was it an organised hit. He was keeping an open mind. They must redouble their efforts to see if Marcus has any enemies, either personally or in his business dealings. He phoned Poirier. "Will you run a double check on both Marcus and Stephanie again just to make sure there are no skeletons in their closet, and no enemies they haven't told us about," "Yes of course sir," "And as soon as possible please,"

Cadieux turned off his computer and took the file home with him hoping against hope that he would spot some vital clue. After a dinner of coq au van and a bottle of red wine, he helped Marie clear the table and then spread out the contents of the file on the empty table. He helped himself to a large cognac and read all of the reports from his team and read the timeline compiled by Lefevre, but with the lack of sightings the timeline was sadly full of holes. The last positive sighting had been in Annecy at Les Glacier des Alps in the afternoon, when they had appeared to be a happy family. Now of course they knew that Alex and Izzy had died, most probably the same day, and before the allotted time to collect Marcus and Stephanie for the party, so the sightings before then had no real relevance.

His phone rang, and this time it was Officer Armand, the forensic officer. "Good evening sir, I have some preliminary news on the crash. The car definitely struck the barriers on the ravine side of the road some distance back. It then careered across the road striking the face of the cliff about 270 meters further on and crossed back over the road before plunging down into the ravine. There are pieces of glass and paint damage at both sites which appear to fit in with the damage to the car. From the distance between the barriers and the cliff face, it appears that the car was travelling about 60 kilometres per hour, not excessive, but with the snow-covered road, it would have been very difficult to control the car once it had started to skid. We will be examining the car to see if it had been struck by another vehicle, but we found no evidence of that on the road. It also appears that the car must have overturned on the road and bounced over the crash barrier where there is paint on the road and on the top edge of the barrier. We have found no evidence as to the cause of the skid," "That is a great help, thank you Armand. Is there a chance that the car could have been pushed over the edge and into the ravine?" "No sir, No chance at all. You will have seen that the barrier on that side of the road was intact, so the car must have gone over the top. That is only possible if the car overturned at some speed," "Yes, I can understand that," "We will be recovering the car first thing in the morning and taking it to our facility in Ecully where it will be thoroughly examined," "Please let me know anything immediately you find it, no matter how small, and at any time, day or night," "Yes sir, of course," And rang off.

Cadieux rang Poirier again. "You can forget that investigation into Marcus' enemies for the time being. It appears the crash could not have been arranged, nor was the car pushed over the edge, so all the evidence now points to a complete accident and an opportunist kidnap, so no point in wasting your time and effort on that. Have an early night and come back refreshed in the morning," "Goodnight sir."

Chapter 35

At H.Q. it was late and much of the building was in darkness. The incident room was empty apart from Detective Lemieux who had recently been appointed as a detective and was staying late at the office going over all of the intelligence that had been submitted to the office. He had a pad on his desk and was looking at the timeline and making notes trying to fit information into different scenarios. He had a small desk light on and had just refilled his coffee mug from the cafetiere in the small kitchen area. He telephoned his wife and told her he was working late in the office and he would be home later. He looked at the pictures of Klara and the crashed car and remembered at his briefing the previous morning the Capitaine had impressed on his team the urgency in finding Klara. "We must step up our game" he had told his men. "Think outside the box. If anyone has any bright ideas, now is the time to make a name for yourself." He tried to think of ways to make a name for himself. What would be the best way to find the kidnapped girl. Probably asking the public for their help. Detective Lemieux was keen to impress the Capitaine with his efficiency, so he sent the pictures of the car and Klara to the television stations and the national newspapers with the report that the car had been found with the bodies of the chauffeur and nanny inside and a request to publish and ask the public for any information on sightings of Klara.

Cadieux poured himself another cognac and pondered this latest information. He was now quite satisfied that this was not a planned abduction and therefore looking for any enemies of Marcus and Stephanie was a waste of resources. He would reassign his team tomorrow morning. It looked for all the world that someone had witnessed the accident, or come across the crashed car, taken Klara from the wreck and kept her. But why keep her so long before making contact. Had they intended to steal her permanently? He knew baby trafficking was a burgeoning business on the internet and a large fee could be paid for a healthy young child. The amount of the ransom demand also concerned him. It was an unusual amount. Why $400,000? Why US dollars? Was this some kind of diversionary tactic. It was certainly creating problems for him. He could not work out exactly what the plans were. It was most infuriating. He looked at the clock in the dining room and saw it was already nearing 2 am. He really needed to get some sleep before the morning briefing, so crept up to bed and tried not to disturb Marie.

Chapter 36

The morning television news channels all carried the kidnap story, photographs of the car and Klara and her picture was in the morning newspapers with the headline "Chaueffeur et Nounou retrouvés morts." A photograph of the Mercedes impaled on the tree in the snow was also being shown. Daniel was eating breakfast in the dining room of the Ibis Hotel Part Dieu Lyon and although he couldn't make out what was being said, he saw the pictures and realised that the Police had found the car and the bodies of Alex and Izzy. He knew that the Police would now be looking for different kidnappers and he would have to slightly alter his plan. Daniels basic French translated morts as dead, recognised Chauffeur and supposed that Nounou meant Nanny. "So," he said to himself, "They now know that Alex and Izzy aren't involved and will be looking elsewhere. I'll have to try to make it more difficult for them."

Cadieux watched the morning television news over breakfast and almost choked. He was fuming and called H.Q. "Who released the information and photographs," "Detective Lemieux sir," "What on earth was he thinking, who have him permission to release that information." "He was only trying to find the girl sir," Cadieux would not be placated. "He is dismissed as a detective, send him back to uniform at once," "Yes sir," "I will be there for the briefing at 7.30 am."

Daniel checked out of the hotel walked into the square and called Lizzie. He told her the news about the discovery of the car and told her not to worry, that he had everything under control. She said that Klara was being an angel and not to worry about them. He told Lizzie to take another picture of Klara and send it to Marcus with the daily paper. Switching on Alex's phone he sent another text to Marcus. *"You have disappointed me. I said no gendarme, but you have not listened. I will send you another picture of Klara this morning in good faith to prove to you that she is well. I did not want you to worry. But now I cannot trust you and I must now reconsider my options,"* Marcus showed the text to Stephanie and forwarded it to Cadieux with the message "I am shocked and horrified at the way in which you are investigating this. You cannot even keep your own officers under control. You have now caused whoever has Klara to not trust us and that puts her in danger. If anything happens to her, I will hold you personally responsible."

Cadieux phoned Police H.Q. and delayed the briefing until 8.30 am and instead went immediately to the chalet where he met an irate Marcus and distraught Stephanie who said "I thought you said you wouldn't do anything that would put Klara in danger. That's just what you and your team have done. If she isn't returned, her blood is on your hands," and weeping, stormed out of the room. Capitaine Cadieux apologised to Marcus, "This happened without my permission. It was a young detective who was trying to impress. I know that doesn't make it any easier to bear, but I will strive to get her back safely. You can be assured of that," "I fully understand that, and I appreciate you and your officers commitment, but it is my daughter that's missing not yours, and we need her back, the sooner the better," "Please let me know if you receive any further texts. I will go back to H.Q. and plan our next tactics," "Tactics, tactics? You don't seem to have any tactics, but you'd better think of some, and quick,"

Cadieux's phone rang. It was the pathologist with the preliminary report on the post-mortems. "No sign of foul play Capitaine. Everything points to the car having left the road and the injuries sustained by the crash. Both bodies sustained severe head injuries, broken ribs, punctured lungs, ruptured spleen and internal bleeding," "Thank you," replied Cadieux and gave Marcus the information, "and that seems to rule out an organised kidnap from any of your potential enemies," "That's good to know, and I assume we are no longer considered suspects," "You never were in that category, it was just we needed to get the full picture, and sometimes we have to ask awkward questions," "I know Officer Benoit is doing an excellent job for us, but I'm also sure that she was your spy," "No Marcus, not a spy, but I did ask her to let me know of anything unusual that she noticed. It is always possible that you had forgotten to mention something which may be significant and if Benoit heard that, she could inform me which could help in finding Klara. The text message for instance," "OK, fair enough. You have your job to do and I understand that it is not an easy one, but you are not as emotionally involved as we are," "You are right up to a point Marcus, but I will tell you that as a young detective I was involved in a kidnapping where the young child was found dead and I vowed then I would never let that happen whilst I was in charge, and to date I have had three successful operations. This one is posing many new challenges, I will admit, but my team of officers is excellent and I am totally confident of bringing Klara back safely," "Thank you for being so honest Cadieux, despite my bad temper now and again, I do have faith in you," "Thank you sir, I appreciate that," replied Cadieux before he left for the briefing.

Chapter 37

Marcus went upstairs to Stephanie who was sobbing uncontrollably on the bed. "I just could not understand why Alex and Izzy would take Klara and ask for a ransom," She sobbed. "I know, I should not have doubted him, but the text came from his phone and it was the obvious answer. The one good thing is that whoever took Klara from the car saved her life, and for that we should be grateful." "I know that, but why won't they let her come home," Stephanie was distraught but pulled herself together to call her father at his hotel. "Daddy, the car has been found and Alex and Izzy are dead, they didn't take Klara, but now the police have messed up. I don't think it was Cadieux's fault but one of their junior officers released important information to the press. I think the kidnappers wanted us to believe that it was Alex and Izzy who had Klara, so now the kidnappers will know that Alex and Izzy are dead and they may want to just cut their losses. What will they do to Klara?" She wailed. "Yes, I know, I saw it on the TV news this morning. Leave it with me, I will speak to the Interior Minister and the Lieutenant who is looking into the case for the Ambassador, then I'll be in touch. Your mother and I will be over shortly. Don't worry, the kidnappers know they have a valuable commodity and won't want to lose that. I'm sure they won't hurt Klara,"

Rutherford called the American Embassy and asked to be put through to Lieutenant Constantine. "Good morning Philip, have you seen the news," "Yes indeed I have, and I have just come off the phone to Capitaine Cadieux who is being very helpful. As you have seen from the television and newspapers, the car has now been found with the bodies of Aleksander and Isabella still in it. I have also spoken to the pathologist this morning and the injuries sustained are not suspicions. It appears likely that your granddaughter was in the car at the time of the crash and has been rescued by someone who has now decided to demand a ransom for her safe return. Not the height of altruism, is it. Cadieux was working on two assumptions, one that Alex and Izzy had orchestrated the kidnap, obviously we now know that was not the case, and second that they had all been abducted by an outside force. The car crash has ruled that theory out as well.

Cadieux is now confident that the crash was an accident, although they cannot find evidence that another vehicle was involved, but it is also quite apparent that your granddaughter would have undoubtedly died in the car from exposure had she not been rescued," "I know, but it leaves a bad taste in the mouth that whoever it was did something so wonderful and have them demean it so badly. I cannot comprehend it at all. It's not that we can't afford the ransom, it's just...just ... I don't know what to say," "I have asked the military if they have any footage of the area on the night of the disappearance and I am waiting for a response. Hopefully this will provide some clue. There are very few CCTV cameras in the area so tracking them at that time is difficult. Our next hope is to track them during the ransom drop," "What technology is available to track the ransom money," "We have to be very careful as we don't want them to get cold feet, pull out and then do something to your granddaughter," "No that would be terrible," "It may depend on the type of ransom drop. We could put a tracker in a bag containing the money, but that could be discovered by an anti-surveillance device which is easily available over the internet, and we don't know what kind of bag they would specify." "What about recording numbers of some of the banknotes of coloured dye or something like that?" "That is possible, yes, although I understand the instructions were for unmarked and non-traceable bills," "How would they know if we just recorded a few numbers?" "Probably not, it is just a risk that's all," "So, are you saying we should just pay the ransom and forget about the money and just be pleased to get Klara back?" "No, not necessarily, but I think we need to hear what the ransom drop arrangements are going to be and the pickup of your grand.... er Klara. That may be our best opportunity to catch them," "Whatever happens it is vital that we get Klara back safe and sound, and if we don't catch them, we don't, and be thankful she is back with us," "I agree. I will keep you up to date with any further information and be assured we will do everything we can," "Thank you Philip,"

He then rang the Interior Minister. "Good morning Dominique, I assume you have heard the news of the car being found," "Yes, I heard this morning from Cadieux. I understand that the young detective has been sent back to the uniform branch, not that that is of any comfort to you, but his career as a detective is probably over," "On reflection Dominique, that is maybe a bit harsh, let him stew for a few months perhaps, but at least he showed some initiative, something that Cadieux seems to lack," "You may be right. However, I am at a loss myself as to where we go from here. Obviously, the kidnappers will now be more wary and we will need to tread carefully. If this is not resolved in the next 48 hours, I will have Cadieux replaced, and maybe a fresh pair of eyes will throw up something he has missed," "Seems like a good idea Dominique. Please keep me informed," "I will Rutherford, Au Revoir,"

Rutherford and Georgina then left their hotel and were driven to the chalet. They met Marcus and Stephanie in the lounge and Rutherford told them what Lieutenant Constantine and the Interior Minister had said. In the depths of despair of the last few days Stephanie had discovered a mental strength she did not know she possessed and had regained her composure. Marcus reported to them all the conversation he had had with Cadieux. They considered all of the information they had been given and discussed their various options. Stephanie then said "I would have lost my darling daughter if it were not for these people. We would now be planning her funeral. I would give every cent of my fortune to have her back with us, so for that I give thanks" Marcus recapped his understanding of their discussions and made his decision. "Whatever the instructions for the ransom drop are, I will follow them to the letter. I will not involve the police at all at that stage. I will not inform them of any of the terms of the ransom or the location of the drop. I will bring my daughter, OUR daughter, back home. Then, and only then, will the police be included," Stephanie hugged him. "I love you Marcus," she said. "And I love you Steph, and Klara, and I will do anything to bring her back to you safely,"

Chapter 38

The morning briefing started a little later than the revised time of 8.30 as Cadieux had still not made it back from the Chalet. He had also first telephoned Lieutenant Constantine at the embassy and asked for an update on the military photographic coverage and had then called the Interior Minister, brought him up to speed on the developments and briefed him on his forthcoming strategy. He opened the briefing meeting with a review of the day's events from yesterday and then "I believe it is now clear that this was not a planned abduction, nor were any of the families involved. The tragic accident and loss of life of Alex and Izzy has given us a set of circumstances I have not had to deal with before, that this is an opportunistic kidnap. Therefore, I am now suspending all enquiries relating to the Meier family and those of Alex and Izzy. British and Polish police are presently informing the next of kin of their deaths. Something I would not like to be doing. I have received information from the American Ambassador's office that their military photographic coverage in the area of the crash site has been unable to provide any conclusive evidence of the preparators of the kidnap or of the reason for the Mercedes to leave the road and crash into the ravine. I now wish to select four of you to look into various options for a potential ransom drop, and another four to prepare options for a rescue of Klara once the ransom has been collected, and to include apprehending the kidnappers. Team A the ransom drop will consist of Rousseau, Dubois, Bertrand and Girard, Team B, the rescue will comprise Laurent, Fournier, Lamy and Poirier, Lefevre will be my conduit, He will collate everything from here, and submit your proposals to me. It appears there are at least two of them working together. Try to think like them, get inside their minds. What is the way they would least expect us to act? Consider all possibilities. Dismiss nothing. All your ideas are welcome"

There was a long pause, then Girard said "Just a thought sir, but now that we know that Alex and Izzy aren't involved, but their phones are being used, have we checked if their chargers are still at the Chalet or in the car. If not, it could be that they might have had to buy chargers," "Well done, Girard. It might be trying to find a needle in a haystack, but it is a possibility. I'll have Benoit check the Chalet and the forensics team can check the car," "Does anyone else have a bright idea like Girard," No one spoke. Cadieux asked Benoit to check the Chalet and a few minutes later reported that Izzy's charger was in her room and it was for a Nokia 8210. Marcus said that Alex always kept his charger in the car. The forensic team did a check on the car but there was no trace of the charger for his Motorola Razr V3.

Cadieux went back into the incident room. "Listen up everyone. Izzy's charger is in her room but Alex's charger is not in the car where it should be. We know that texts have been received in Marseilles, and Lyon, quite large cities, but if we can find out when and where an 8210 charger was bought, we might have a lead. See what you can do," Fournier spoke up, "Sir I've looked at the text from Izzy's phone which was sent in Lyon at 11.55 a.m," "Yes" "But the photograph was time stamped at 10.18 a.m. the same day," "Mmm" "Why would you wait more than an hour and a half to send the photo and the text?" "Why indeed," "I think they took the photo at a different location to throw us off the scent sir," "I think you may be right Fournier. We need to find the location where the photo was taken. Are there any clues in the photo itself?" "I haven't seen any sir," "An hour and a half travelling is a fairly large area to cover, but let's draw a circle around Lyon and see where it takes us. Do we have a definite location in Lyon where the text came from?" "Yes sir, the mobile company have only been able to estimate the position from two masts and have sent us the co-ordinates to within about 800 metres. The closest they could get was 45.41 N and 4.57 E towards the South east corner of Lyon," "OK, I would think that they would not want to get caught up in the morning traffic in Lyon, so they probably approached from the South round to the East of Lyon. Allowing for an average speed of say 75 Kilometres per hour at that time of day, we could draw a circle of no more than 110 to 150 km from those coordinates. What is included in that circle?" Fournier checked his road atlas. "Probably, erm.. Valence round through Grenoble, Chambery, Aix-les-Bains and Annecy are all possible sir," "Annecy again, right then, contact all the police departments in those districts and have them start checking vehicles that may contain one or two adults with a small child. If necessary, put out road blocks," "Yes sir," Cadieux was starting to feel a little more upbeat, that the tide was turning and he was homing in on the kidnappers.

Chapter 39

Daniel sent a text to Marcus,
Text the registration number of your car.
Marcus saw the text almost immediately and replied with the information. He then received another text,
Drive from Chamonix to Gare Lyon Part Deux with the money in a brief case. When you arrive in Lyon send a text to say you have arrived. You will then receive further instructions. Make sure you are alone and no-one is following you. Park at the left-hand end of the car park against the fence and sit in the car until notified. If there is any sign of police the handover will be cancelled. You will be watched.
Daniel switched off the Razr phone and called Lizzie on his Nokia, "OK, he is moving, are you ready?" "Yes, we're both sitting in the van ready to go." "Right, go to Saxe-Gambetta and wait there with the carrier bag."

Marcus had had another car delivered to them several days ago, so was able to make a start immediately. Stephanie said "Please be careful Darling." "Don't worry, I will be safe. And I will bring back Klara to you, to us." So, he left for Lyon.

Officer Benoit called Cadieux, "Sir, Marcus has just left the chalet on his own with a large holdall." "Looks like he is going to make a drop and hasn't told me, thank you Benoit." Cadieux called Girard over to him. "Is there any way you can track the car?" "With a bit more time I could have arranged the gendarmerie patrol cars to be in positions, to spot him, I could try, but we don't know which direction her is travelling in do we." "No, from the previous text messages, my educated guess would be south towards Marseilles and Lyon. Can you see if there is a patrol car somewhere on the A6 that could keep a lookout?" "Yes sir, that seems like a distinct possibility. I'll get straight onto it." 40 minutes later Girard called to Cadieux, "He's on the A6 Capitaine, travelling south, good thinking. Do you want him followed?" "Yes please, but do not stop him." Girard passed on the order to the gendarmerie.

It would take Marcus about two and a half hours depending on traffic and weather conditions to reach Lyon. Marcus was thinking about Cadieux. He was certain that the policeman would not give up easily, but he was also focused on his own outcome, Klara's safety. He was keeping a watchful eye out for any sign of police cars. He had been driving for almost an hour when he noticed a police patrol car in his rear-view mirror. Marcus checked his speed and saw it was 110 kmph. Spot on to the speed limit. He kept checking on the police car and saw it stayed the same distance behind him, so he slowed imperceptibly down to 95. The police car stayed behind him. After two or three kilometres he increased speed back up to 110. The police car stayed there as well. There was a service area coming up in 10 km, so he pulled in there. The police car also pulled in and parked some distance away from him.

Marcus took out his mobile and called Cadieux. When Cadieux answered, Marcus said "Call him off NOW." "Marcus, we are only trying to help." "Help getting Klara killed perhaps. I told you no interference. If I see another police vehicle following me, I will just turn round and call off the drop. Do I make myself clear? BACK OFF." "Of course Mr Meier, as you wish." Marcus ended the call and waited. Two or three minutes passed then the police car pulled out of the service area and onto the A6 heading south. Marcus followed and at the next exit, the police car pulled off the A6 and turned north.

Arriving at the station car park Marcus sent a text that he had arrived. Daniel had parked the Citroen and sat watching the car park from a distance. He saw the car arrive and texted,
Open the boot fully, then all doors wide open. Wait for one minute then close all doors and the boot and leave your car unlocked, bring the briefcase and walk to the Part Dieu Villete Sud light rail station. If there is any sign of police, the handover will not take place. Take the Metro Line B train heading south to Oullins Centre. Get on the last carriage and send text that you have boarded. You are still being watched.
Marcus did as he was told and walked up to the light rail station. He tried to carefully look around to see who was watching him, but couldn't see anyone suspicious. Obviously, he thought to himself, they are not going to look suspicious. Marcus boarded the last carriage of the southbound train heading for Oullins and texted his reply. Immediately he had another text.
Get off at the Saxe-Gambetta station. Go to street level. You will see a carrier bag under the bench outside the boulangerie with a box inside with message on the lid.
Lizzie had driven to Saxe-Gambetta and was sitting in the camper waiting for Daniels text. As soon as she received his text she locked and left the camper with Klara playing with her toys, and sat on the bench with a carrier bag at her feet. As soon as she saw Marcus

leaving the station she got up from the bench and got back into the camper van, started up and drove away. As she did so a grey Citroen Saxa pulled into her parking space. At Saxe-Gambetta Marcus had left the train and raced up the steps to street level. He hurried to the bench, took the box out of the carrier bag and read the message taped to the lid.

Chapter 40

Marcus, take the mobile out of the box and read the instructions on the paper in the box.
He opened the box and read the computer printed message.
You are being watched. Do not contact Cadieux or the gendarme. Leave your mobile in the box in the carrier bag under the bench. It will be returned to you. All new messages will be on this phone. Go back into the Metro, and take the Line D train to Gare de Venissieux. Remember you are being watched.
Marcus put his mobile in the box, left it as instructed, and entered the Metro. Daniel collected the bag from under the bench as soon as Marcus disappeared into the Metro. He was wearing a hoodie and driving gloves and placed the mobile into a plastic bag, destroyed the box and message and put everything into his holdall. He then drove off to Monplaisir-Lumiere to wait for Marcus to arrive. The new phone bleeped with an incoming message from a withheld number.
Marcus do not board the first train. Wait for the second train.
Marcus let the first Line D train pass then boarded the next train and a few moments after it had left the station another text arrived.
Leave the train at Monplaisir-Lumière walk to the bandstand in the centre of the park. Sit on a bench and wait there.
Marcus carefully looked around the carriage at the other passengers. There were only seven. Two were elderly men, one was an old woman three were young men in the twenties or thirties and one schoolgirl. All of them appeared engrossed in either reading a

newspaper or book or were looking at their mobile phone. No-one was looking at him.

Marcus arrived at Monplaisir-Lumiere station and was the only one to get off the train. He saw the bandstand just a few metres away. It was hexagonal with a low fence running around it and four or five benches. He walked to it and look around and sat at a bench. A text arrived from the withheld number.

Unfortunately, the involvement of Capitaine Cadieux and the gendarme have caused me a slight problem. You may keep the cash in the briefcase. There is no intention of increasing the amount requested. I want you to know that Klara is safe and happy. I now need you to call your bank and arrange a transfer of $400,000 to a numbered bank account which is written on the piece of paper taped to the back of the phone. As soon as the funds have cleared, Klara will be returned to you safe, well and unharmed. I am truly sorry for all of the stress caused to you and Stephanie.

The tone of the text confused Marcus. He was angry at his daughter having been kidnapped of course, and was angry at having to pay a ransom for her safe return, but it did not seem to fit with the text he had received, which appeared to be very apologetic. He did not dare to speak to Cadieux in case it backfired and Klara was hurt in any way, so, fortunately he knew his bank's phone number, and speaking to the manager asked him to arrange the immediate transfer of the ransom demand to the account number on the piece of paper.

The manager was immediately concerned for Marcus and Stephanie and the safety of Klara. "How do you know your daughter will be released once the money is transferred," "I have no proof of course, but he has told me to keep the $400,000 in cash and Klara has always appeared to be happy and well cared for in the photographs, so I must trust him. I don't know what else I can do," "The bank account is in an offshore account and we have no way of recalling the funds once it is transferred. We also have no way of contacting the bank," "I understand that and I trust that you will carry out my instructions to the letter," "Of course, Herr Meier, it is almost closing time at the bank, but I will see to it personally that the transfer will take place." "I will of course be returning the $400,000 cash that you provided," Marcus then sent a text to Daniel.

I have spoken to the bank manager and the bank transfer is taking place now, please, please tell me where Klara is.

Daniel responded

Go back to the metro and take the Line D train to Laënnec. Leave the train and walk to the Square Thomas Blanchet and wait for further instructions, as soon as the funds have cleared I will text the location of Klara.

Chapter 41

Having been notified of the clearance of the funds, Daniel texted Marcus. Funds have cleared. *There is a litter bin beside one of the entrances. Drop this mobile into the litter bin and return to your car. You are being watched. I will send a text with the location of Klara to your own mobile.* Return to your car. Your mobile is in a plastic bag under the car with the location of Klara who is happy and well and looking forward to be with her mummy and daddy again. He then texted Lizzie Funds cleared, see you soon, and drove off to the Part Dieu Villete Sud light rail station. Lizzie was parked at the Square Thomas Blanchet and saw Marcus drop the mobile into the waste bin. Waiting until he had gone back to the Metro, she jumped out of the van and picked up the mobile from the bin. She then sent a text to Daniel.

I have the mobile.

Daniel was wearing a hoodie which he pulled the hood up over his head. He parked at the car park at Gare Lyon Part Deux and carrying the carrier bag he carefully checked that no one was watching him.

As he passed Marcus' car, he bent down, placed the carrier bag with the mobile in under the car by the rear wheel. He straightened up and continued on to the station. He looked at the destination board and saw that there was almost an hour before the next train to Marseilles. He bought a ticket to Marseilles and put it in his pocket. He bought a coffee at the coffee shop and stood beside the doors where he could see Marcus' car. After about 5 minutes he saw Marcus hurrying across from the light rail station. He got to his car and looked underneath. He retrieved the carrier bag, took out his phone and read the text from Alex's phone.

Chapter 42

Lizzie had been waiting for the text from Daniel and was sitting outside a patisserie at Place Guichard-Bourse du Travail. It was at a junction of six streets, with a small tree lined park and there were several tables and benches where people were enjoying an early evening coffee and chatting. Lizzie was wearing her hooded top pulled up, while Klara sitting beside her, was happily demolishing a large piece of chocolate cake, most of which appeared to be spread around her face, with a milk shake. Lizzie was a mess. She had enjoyed the time she had spent with Klara, and had loved looking after her, but it was now time to let her go back to her parents. She took out her phone and took a picture of Klara eating the chocolate cake and sent it to Daniel. She felt her heart was breaking as she looked at the little one enjoying her cake and milk shake, and found herself being very emotional and had to hold back tears. Daniel sent a text to Marcus' phone with the picture of Klara.

Drive to Place Guichard-Bourse du Travail. At the crossroads there is a patisserie with tables and benches outside where Klara is enjoying chocolate cake and a milk shake.

Daniel drove to Place Guichard-Bourse du Travail and saw Lizzie sitting at the bench. He crossed over the road and went to them.

"Hi Klara," and gave her a hug. "Would you like another piece of cake." Klara, her face already covered in chocolate, grinned back at him. Daniel and Lizzie walked into the patisserie, and while Daniel watched from the door, Lizzie bought two coffees and pieces of cake and sat down at a table with tears in her eyes. Daniel saw Marcus walking, no running, into the square and then he saw Klara. "Klara" he yelled. Heads turned and Klara saw him and cried "Daddy." Marcus picked up Klara in his arms and squeezed her tightly to his chest, kissing her with chocolate and tears all over his face. Marcus said to the people sitting at the next table "Excusez-moi, avez-vous vu qui était avec elle?"

(Excuse me did you see who was sitting with her) "Votre femme était ici il y a quelques instants" (*Your wife was here a few moments ago*).

Marcus looked around but there was no trace of anyone else. Carrying Klara, he hurried back to the metro and to his car.

Daniel turned away from the door and sat beside Lizzie, tears also running down his face. They made an effort to eat the cake but it was forming a huge lump in their throats, unable to speak to each other. They waited almost half an hour, their coffee left on the table completely cold. Then they left, Daniel going to the Citroën and Lizzie to their lonely camper. "See you in Paris Lizzie," he said.

Chapter 43

Marcus got back to his car, retrieved his phone and called Stephanie. "Darling, here's Klara to talk to you, say hello to Mummy Klara." "Hi sweetheart, Mummy here, are you alright." "Hello Mummy" and Klara started crying. "Daddy will bring you home now sweetheart," then to Marcus "Are you ok, did everything work out alright." "Well, I have Klara which is the most important thing. I can't wait to get back home to you. I'll tell you all about it then. I'm going to phone Cadieux now and let him know." "Thank you Darling, I love you." "And I love you too."

Marcus then rang Cadieux. "I now have Klara back safe and sound. I am in Lyon and am driving back to Chamonix now." "That is excellent news, I assume you made a ransom drop which you did not tell me about." "Yes, that was my decision. Klara's safety was more important to me than anything else. I will give you all of the details tomorrow morning if you would come to the chalet, but the cash is still in my car. He made me issue a bank transfer to an offshore account because of your involvement." "If you give me the details, I will get our experts to see if they can track it." "I'm sorry, I don't really remember them they were written down on another mobile and I had to leave that in a waste bin. My bank is now closed, so I won't be able to get that information until tomorrow morning." "Very well, that is unfortunate. I will see you at 8 a.m. at the chalet tomorrow."

Daniel pulled into an Aire just north of Lyon and logged on to his bank account. He saw the balance of $400,000. He immediately started moving the funds, in parcels, from bank to bank in the Seychelles, Hong Kong, Belize and Panama. He then transferred the whole balance to a bank in the Cayman Islands and closed the other accounts. This whole operation took the best part of an hour. He hoped that this would be sufficient to conceal their identity. He realised that it would take almost six hours to reach Paris, then drove off towards Orly airport, stopping at another Aire on the A6 where he reconnected the speedometer. Then he drove into the Orly airport car park found the parked car, which was fortunately still there, and changed the number plates back again. He then drove back to his hotel beside the Gare du Lyon and went to bed where Lizzie was waiting for him and they fell into an exhausted sleep in each other's arms.

Chapter 44

Daniel woke early, crept out of bed trying not to wake Lizzie, got washed and dressed and returned the car to the hire company. "You haven't done many kilometres sir," said the agent. "No that's true, but Paris is such a small city, and to see the sites was easier than I expected. Anyway, no damage to the car so that is also a bonus." "Thank you for your custom sir, and we hope to see you again." "Maybe next year. Thank you," and Daniel returned to the hotel where Lizzie had just finished dressing. "I've taken the car back, so after breakfast, it's back home." "Do you think we've got away with it?" "Well, it won't be for the want of trying, but whatever happens I'll keep you in the clear."

At 8 am sharp, Cadieux, accompanied by Lieutenant Laurent, rang the bell at the chalet. He was greeted by Marcus who had Klara tightly grasping his hand. "Capitaine Cadieux, please allow me to introduce the cause of all your troubles of the last week or so. Klara, this is the nice man who has been looking for you." Cadieux bent down and smiled at Klara. "It's very nice to meet you Klara." Klara hid behind her Daddies leg and shyly peeked out at the Capitaine who said "Marcus, this is my senior detective Lieutenant Pierre Laurent, I would like him to be present at this debriefing in case he thinks of something I might miss." "Of course, Cadieux, Lieutenant you are more than welcome. Please come in. Would you like coffee perhaps." "That would be most welcome Marcus, thank you."

They followed Marcus and Klara, still hanging on tightly to her father's hand, into the lounge where Stephanie was waiting. "Good morning Capitaine. A much more pleasant meeting than our previous ones I think." "For both of us Stephanie, for both of us, this is my senior detective Pierre Laurent whom I would like to join us." "Please take a seat while I make some coffee." "Marcus," Cadieux began, "what can you tell us about the handover of the ransom and the pick-up of Klara." "Not much really. I am assuming it was a he, although I am sure a woman was involved. He made me switch phones, leaving mine in a carrier bag, blaming it on your involvement and all future messages were to that phone from a withheld number. I had to use several trains on the Lyon Metro system, then left the new phone in a waste bin. After the funds were cleared at the bank, he sent a text to my own phone which had been left under my car with Klara's location. When I went there and found Klara eating chocolate cake, I asked people sitting at the next table of anyone has been with her they said your wife was here a moment ago. That's why I think a woman was also involved." Stephanie brought in coffee and took Klara to her room, away from the interview. Cadieux and Laurent then spent the next three hours going over the whole afternoon, almost on a minute-by-minute basis, sometimes asking the same questions twice or even three times. It was surprising to Marcus how this intense questioning was forcing him to remember small details, which he did not think he knew.

They did stop for a break just after 10 a.m. and Stephanie replenished the coffee pot. Marcus was glad he had not committed a crime, as he felt under so much pressure from the experienced detective's incessant questioning, he felt sure he would have confessed to a murder if they had asked him. Finally, Cadieux said "Marcus, that has been a great help. I am sure you feel that the return of Klara has closed the case for you, but for me it is only half a case and I will try to find the perpetrators and bring them to justice. I understand you are leaving Chamonix today and returning to Lausanne." "Yes that's right, the stress of this holiday means I can go back to work for a rest. I hope you are successful in catching the criminals. Goodbye Cadieux, and thank you and your team for all of your efforts." Cadieux and Laurent then left the chalet and returned to police H.Q. to begin the search.

Daniel and Lizzie walked back to the camper van and Daniel drove into the centre of Paris and found a parking space in Rue de la Paix in Place Vendôme. He jumped out of the camper, "come on Lizzie" Lizzie looked bemused, but got out of the camper. She followed him along the street and he stopped at No 9 and looked into the window of Mellerio, reputed to be the oldest jeweller in Paris. The Mellerios had settled in France from Italy in 1515 but in 1613 Queen Marie de Medicis granted them privileges to practice in France without having to submit to the generally applied administrative restrictions, as a reward for foiling a plot against her son Louis XVI. Their clients have included Marie Antoinette, Queen Josephine, Napoleon III and his wife Empress Eugênie. "Apparently this is where the best people come to buy their engagement rings." Lizzie looked in awe at the collection of rings in the shop window. "Are we buying an engagement ring Daniel?" "I think we should make it official Lizzie, but only if you really want to, and I want you to know that I am using my grandmothers inheritance to buy the ring. Let's go in shall we?"

So in they went and were met by a smartly dressed man, probably in his mid to late forties. "Parlez-vous anglais s'il vous plait." "Oui Monsieur, but of course. My name is Henri, how can I help you?" "My fiancée would like to look at engagement rings." "Certainly sir, and may I offer you both my congratulations." "Thank you," they both said. "Please take a seat, and would you like coffee?" "Yes please, that would be lovely," and two chairs had miraculously appeared behind them. "What kind of ring would you like Lizzie?" asked Daniel. "I think I would like a diamond set in emeralds." "An excellent choice mademoiselle if I may say so, that will match your hair and eyes perfectly." They sat down and Henri and his assistant brought trays of engagement rings for their approval, some of which Lizzie thought were way out of their league, after all they were still only students, despite Daniels inheritance and she did not want to appear ostentatious. Daniel insisted that she chose the ring

137

she liked, and after trying on several, decided on the final one. It wasn't too expensive, fitted the size of Lizzies hand perfectly and more importantly Lizzie loved it. The ring needed to be slightly resized and they were given more coffee while they waited for the alteration to be made.

They returned to the camper, Lizzies head in the clouds, and her left hand feeling very strange with the beautiful ring on her third finger. They walked a few doors down and Daniel went into the Park Hyatt and booked a room. They arranged for valet parking and drove the camper to the entrance and handed over the keys to the concierge. They were shown to their room which was very spacious and showered and changed before going down to the bar for aperitifs then into the restaurant for dinner. Lizzie had chosen to eat at Café Jeanne and Daniel had ordered a bottle of champagne, which was chilling by their table. Lizzie ordered Duck foie gras confit, followed by Pan seared sea bass with green asparagus. Daniel chose 6 Tarbouriech Oysters in escabeche sauce and Simmental beef fillet with three peppers and mashed potatoes. They had a glass of Beaune with their first course, Lizzie had a second glass of Beaune with her sea bass and Daniel preferred a glass of Pauillac with his steak. They both chose crème brûleé for dessert and Daniel also asked for a selection of cheeses. Their coffee arrived and Lizzie had a glass of port while Daniel had a cognac. "Daniel, that was absolutely gorgeous, thank you." "I'm only getting engaged once, so I'm celebrating with the most wonderful girl in the world." Lizzie laughed, "and when is she going to turn up?" And Daniel knew then he had picked the right girl for him. They took the remains of the champagne and went back to their room to celebrate.

The next morning after a late breakfast they left Paris and headed for the Eurotunnel terminal at Calais, first on the A1 and then on the A26. They had enjoyed a good breakfast, so managed to make the journey without stopping and were able to book a crossing at 4.45 p.m. They spent time in the duty-free shop and stocked up on perfume and toiletries for Lizzie and alcohol and after shave for Daniel, who also, although, not a smoker, took a stock of cigarettes for his student friends. They loaded the camper onto the Eurotunnel and just after 5.25 they drove onto British soil, passed through customs and onto the A2.

Chapter 45

Back on Teesside, the first thing Lizzie wanted to do was phone her Mam. "Hi Mam, we're back." "Hello Lizzie, did you have a good time?" "Well, you could say that. We got engaged." "What?" her mother screamed in delight. "That's marvellous, just wait until your Dad gets home. I can't wait to tell him. Are you going out to look for a ring?" "No, we bought one on Paris." "When can you come over to see us?" "We were thinking of this weekend, is that OK?" "Of course it is. Obviously Paris worked its magic on you." "Yes, I'll tell you everything when I see you on Friday night." "Wait 'till I tell your brothers. You're not giving up university, are you? this isn't going to affect your career, is it?" "No Mam, Daniel is very keen for me to be a doctor, and he is working on his software, so I won't give up easily." "I can't wait to see you on Friday Lizzie." "Me too Mam, love to Dad and the boys. Bye." "Bye."

Daniel was also keen to phone his parents and his Dad answered the phone. "Hi Dad, got a bit of news for you, I'm engaged." "To Lizzie?" "Yes Dad, to Lizzie, who else would have me." "I'm very pleased for you son, congratulations, Abigail," he shouted, "Daniels on the phone," then quietly "You tell your mum yourself; she'll like that." Abigail came to the phone "Hello Daniel, had a good time?" "Very good Mum, Lizzie and I are engaged." "That's fantastic news son, I like Lizzie, she's lovely and I hope you'll both be very happy." "Well, if we are as happy as you two seem to be we should be fine."

"That's nice to know, although you should check that out with your father, he might have a different opinion," and she laughed. "Mum, you don't mean that." "No of course I don't, we've got a good life together and I hope it also works out for you. It can be hard from time-to-time mind, it's not all plain sailing. When are you bringing Lizzie to see us again?" "Well, we are planning to go to Manchester on Friday for the weekend, so are you free the following weekend." "We are now, whatever we have on we'll cancel, and we'll take both of you out for dinner on Saturday to celebrate. We'll go to that nice pub in Haywards Heath that you like, what's it called?" "Don't you mean The Thatched Inn at Hassocks?" "Yes, that's the one, not Haywards Heath, shall I book it?" "That'll be great Mum." "I'll pass you back to your Dad, he wants to say something, Bye son, and I'm delighted." "Bye Mum." "Just wanted to say I think you've got yourself I cracker, look after her son," said Barry. "Will do Dad, Bye."

Chapter 46

Having returned to the North East, Daniel realised that both the police and Marcus would have long memories and may well continue searching for them for some years so he tried to make plans for this eventuality. Following the movement of the ransom money through various banks and countries, Daniel had finally invested the money in the Cayman Islands. He had created new identities for each of them in the Caymans and, although it had taken time, had obtained Cayman Islands passports under their new assumed name of Daniel and Elizabeth Seymour. They had considered changing their Christian names, but thought that it would be easier to make a mistake with different first names. He had formed several companies in the Cayman Islands and was developing and marketing his computer gaming software from three of those companies, each of which was a subsidiary of a holding company, whose main shareholders were Daniel and

Elizabeth Seymour. He opened bank accounts for each company in different banks, each with a substantial balance and obtained credit cards for them from American Express and Barclaycard and debit cards from each of the banks. Whilst he was uncertain whether the police would be able to track them down after the ransom had been paid, he was trying to cover his tracks and the sooner he did that the better. Daniel explained his plan to Lizzie and then put the plans into action..

Chapter 47

Cadieux was frustrated. Whilst he was delighted that Klara had been found, he was disappointed that he hadn't caught the kidnappers. Yet. Marcus invited all of the team of detectives who had searched for Klara to Lausanne and laid on transport and hotel rooms for each of them, including their partners to join them. He even invited Officer Lemieux and his wife, much to the consternation of Capitaine Cadieux, however Marcus felt that the issue of the information to the press had moved the search forward, so he insisted that Lemieux was invited. Marcus and Stephanie were delighted to have their daughter back safe and sound and had booked a private room at the Beau-Rivage Palace, a five-star hotel set in its own grounds of 10 acres. The elegant belle époque buildings of the Beau-Rivage Palace commanded breath-taking views across Lake Geneva to the majestic French Alps beyond.

The luxury coach that Marcus had hired deposited his guests in the late morning, where they had a light lunch, checked into their rooms and were able to wander the grounds in the afternoon. The spa was also available and many ladies took advantage of that, something that for many was a first-time experience. Dinner was to be served at 8 p.m. and at 7 o'clock the guests started arriving at the bar where drinks and canapes were served. Marcus and

Stephanie mingled with the police officers and their partners and getting their insights into the operation. All of the officers were pleased at the outcome of Klara being released, but tinged with professional regret that the kidnappers were still at large. After the meal, Marcus stood up and tapped his wine glass with a spoon. The hum of conversation died away. "Ladies and Gentlemen, welcome to this celebration, and it is a celebration. I salute you, each and every one of you for your contributions to the safe return of our daughter Klara, who unfortunately cannot be with us tonight as she is otherwise engaged in her bedroom, dreaming of, I know not what. I know that you all feel to some extent deflated because the kidnappers have not been apprehended." "Yet," Fournier again with the interjection. "That's as maybe," continued Marcus smiling, "and I understand and agree with you to some extent, however, I will ask you to consider this. You all know that I have been extremely fortunate in my life and have accumulated a substantial amount of money, and you of all people, officer Lefevre know that, having been through my bank statements with a fine toothcomb," everyone laughed and Lefevre reddened. "But my point is, that if you had the money that Stephanie and I are lucky enough to have, would you not give $400,000 for the safe return of your daughter, or would you rather bury her in the ground having frozen or starved to death in that ravine, and live for the rest of your lives with the torment of knowing how she died. We have come to terms with the payment of the money, and yes it hurts to think of it sometimes, but I only have to look at Klara running around in our house and all of that hurt goes away. I thank you all, no, WE thank you all, from the bottom of our hearts for your efforts in trying to find her, and I hope that you can take comfort from our acceptance of the situation as it now is. Thank you, in my mind, for a successful operation." And sat down to a round of applause. Stephanie sitting beside him squeezed his arm and had tears in her eyes. "That was beautiful," she said.

When they married, Elizabeth had retained her EU passport in her maiden name, had continued to work as a junior doctor as Elizabeth Wells and had decided to drop Lizzie as her name, now preferring to be called Elizabeth, although Daniel sometimes did use it affectionately. Daniel still had his EU passport as Daniel Hodge. The longer this subterfuge went on the safer Daniel felt. However, that was about to change

Chapter 48

Cadieux was frustrated. He had joined his fellow officers on the trip to Lausanne and had chatted with Stephanie and Marcus at the Hotel. He understood the sentiment behind Marcus' speech, but his overriding aim was to catch criminals and it didn't sit easily with him that on this occasion he had not. He and Marie had enjoyed the two days they had spent in Lausanne, and it had certainly been a worthwhile bonding experience for him and the rest of his team, but the kidnappers had got away, and whichever way he looked at it, in his eyes the operation was a failure. He had failed to catch the kidnappers. Yes, Klara had been released, not by his doing, but by the kidnappers doing. They had taken the money and given Klara back, as they had said they would, safe and unharmed. They had kept their word. She was home with her parents. So why was he so frustrated. Because he had not done his job. He had not caught the kidnappers, and no matter how Marcus dressed it up with his fine speech, nothing of which he could disagree with, he was angry with himself for not doing his job. I have failed. Failed, he told himself.

He had talked to Marie about it and she had tried to console him with the same reasoning that Marcus had used, but to no avail. He would not, could not, be consoled. He read the file every night, trying to find the chink, the one thing that would point him in the right direction, but try as he might he could not find it. He asked for an appointment with his senior officer, and asked if he should resign. "Why would you want to do that?" the officer replied. "I have failed. The kidnappers got away. It is eating into my brain why could I not catch them?" The officer was kind and said "Are you trying to say that you are infallible? Do you think that you are God?" "No sir I am not." "Then accept that you are human, and for once, the other man won. You are a fine respected police officer with an excellent record, Your success rate is far better than most, but you must let this go. I don't blame you; nobody blames you. Take some time off, take Marie away on holiday, relax, or even get drunk, and come back and crack the next case like you have before." "Thank you sir, maybe that's what I need." Cadieux left the office, went home and he and Marie booked a holiday cruising the Greek islands.

Part II 2011

Chapter 49

"What have we here. There there. Don't worry, I'll look after you. Are you going to be my brave little girl"? At the sound of the doctor's voice, Klara stopped crying, her eyes opened wide, and stared at the doctor. Stephanie was astonished, and looked at the doctor in surprise. Yes, thought Klara, she can look after me,
She will look after me,
She did look after me.
Elizabeth smiled at the child, thought she saw recognition in her eyes, picked up the clipboard with the registration form and looked at the name
Klara Meier
Klara?

Klara!!

Her eyes opened wide and she felt the blood drain from her face. She dropped the clipboard with a crash onto the floor, her legs gave way and she fell against the bed. Stephanie and Emilie were astonished. "Are you alright." They asked and Emilie rushed around the bed to help her. Elizabeth recovered her composure and said weekly, "Yes, I'm fine thank you, I'm pregnant and I feel faint every now and then." "Sit down and I'll get you some water." They hadn't noticed, but now that her doctors coat was hanging open, they could see that in a few more weeks there would be another addition to the global population explosion. Elizabeth sat down and thankfully drank the water Emilie had poured for her. She was trying to calm the raging panic in her head, thinking rapidly what to do. I'm sure Klara recognises me she thought. How am I going to deal with that? She pulled herself together, stood up, and went back to Klara. "Now then, I'm sorry about that, Klara isn't it, now how did you manage to do this." "I fell off a roundabout Iz….". She'd was about to say more but Elizabeth abruptly cut her off, being very officious. "Well, I think we'd better get your arm x-rayed. That head wound looks nasty and it will need to be stitched, but we'll soon get you sorted out. How on earth did you fall off the roundabout." "I was on the roundabout and it was going quite slowly, then some boys started pushing it really really fast. I tried to hold on but I got dizzy and then I woke up with Emilie bending down beside me on the ground and my arm hurt." "Do you not remember falling off the roundabout?" "I don't think so. I remember whizzing around and around, but I must have let go 'cos I got dizzy." "Don't worry, I'll get a porter to take you down to the x-ray department." "Will you take me please?" said Klara. "I'll walk down with you, but I can't push the trolley, That's a porter's job."

Elizabeth left the cubicle to call for the porter. She was shaking and was trying to control her nerves. She waited at the nurses station until the porter arrived and he, Elizabeth, on very shaky legs and holding Klara's hand, Stephanie and Emilie made their way to the x-Ray department. Elizabeth walked over to the desk and talked to the receptionist. After a short wait, the radiologist called Klara's name and came to collect Klara. "Come with me please," Klara asked Elizabeth. "I'm sorry but I'm not allowed in there." She replied. "Why not" "Well Klara, it's because I'm having a baby and the x-rays would harm the baby." and the radiologist wheeled the trolley into the x-ray room. Elizabeth said to Stephanie "Please excuse me, I'm sorry I don't feel very well. I almost fainted back in the cubicle. Tell Klara I'm very sorry, but another doctor will come and see her," and she walked down the corridor to the locker room.

Opening her locker, she pulled out her mobile phone and speed dialled her husband. When he answered she said, "Daniel, were in trouble. Klara has been brought into A&E and she's recognised me." "Christ Almighty! Are you sure? You'd better get out of there fast, and hope she forgets you. Can you leave now, blame it on the baby?" "I think I'll have to. I nearly fainted when I saw her name on the clipboard. Nearly passed out. God, what are we going to do Daniel?" "First of all, were going to stay calm. Not get ahead of ourselves." "I thought we were clear after all this time. Everything behind us, and now this comes back to bite us." "You just get yourself home now. I will leave my office now and then we'll talk it over tonight. Love you sweetheart." "Love you to, see you soon." Elizabeth then left the locker room, reported sick to the A&E duty manager, and left the hospital.

Chapter 50

As Klara was taken back to the cubicle from having her arm x-rayed, Marcus arrived at the hospital from the Embassy looking very worried. Stephanie went to him and explained what had happened. "What was Emilie thinking about, not looking after her," he asked angrily. "That's not fair Marcus, and you know it. Children need to play and explore and that is exactly what Klara was doing. It wasn't her fault; I think some boys started spinning the roundabout too fast after she got on. We were both watching and she seemed to be holding on just fine and then she must have lost her grip or something. We can't, and I won't, wrap her up in cotton wool, just because of what happened years ago. Emilie and I were only a few yards away chatting, but still watching her. Emilie was great with Klara after the accident, very efficient, so I don't expect you to be angry with her OK." Marcus was somewhat taken aback by Stephanie's outburst and meekly said "Ok Darling, if that's what you want, I'll say nothing more," and went over to see Klara. "How are you mein Kliener, that was a silly thing to do wasn't it." "Yes Daddy, I fell off a roundabout but Izzy is looking after me." "That's good Klara, does it hurt." "Yes, a little bit, but only when I try to move my arm." "Well then, don't try to move it. That's your body's way of telling you to keep it still." "Yes Daddy, did you see Izzy." "No sweetheart I didn't."

Marcus went over to Stephanie and said, "She said Izzy was looking after her." Stephanie frowned, "that's odd, and a little worrying." "I agree, she also asked if I'd seen her." A nurse came in holding the x-ray results. "The doctors' have had a look at these and we need to put your arm in a plaster cast." she said. "It won't hurt a bit and you can get all of your friends to sign their names on it. You'll be quite the centre of attention. Then I'm afraid we'll have to keep you in overnight for observation." "Why is that? we can look after her," asked Stephanie. "I'm sure you can but she took a nasty fall and was unconscious for a short time, so we need to make sure there is nothing more serious than the cut, and that will have to be stitched." "Where is she." Klara asked the nurse. "Where's who?" "Izzy" "Who?" "The other lady doctor, Izzy". "Dr Wells wasn't feeling well, she's expecting a baby and it probably turned, it happens all the time, but her name isn't Izzy its Elizabeth." "He called her that." "Who did" "The snowman, he called her Izzy." "No love, you must be mistaken, her name is not Izzy it is Elizabeth. I think that bump on your head must be worse than we thought. We'd better keep you in for a couple of days rather than just overnight."

So, Klara was taken to the plaster room where a nice white plaster cast was wrapped round her arm and then wheeled up to the children's ward. There were lots of children in the ward, some confined to their beds, but others in the playroom playing with many of the toys donated to the hospital. Stephanie and Emilie stayed with Klara, but Marcus returned to the Embassy for a scheduled zoom meeting with Chancellor Merkel, and soon Klara was off to play in the playroom with the other children. "Stephanie, who is Izzy?" asked Emilie. "It's rather sad actually, Izzy was a nanny for Klara when she was almost three, but she died in an accident. I thought Klara had got over it, but maybe it is more deep seated than we thought."

Chapter 51

When Daniel returned home Elizabeth was sitting in the lounge weeping. "We are going to prison Daniel" she wailed. "No, we aren't sweetheart, just call in sick and then we'll bring forward our move to the States. We can find a nice house or condo or something, somewhere nice and warm. I can continue to develop my software from there, and you can take it easy until the baby arrives. It's almost time for your maternity leave anyway. You can hand in your resignation due to my having to leave for America and no-one will have second thoughts about you and Klara. Get your resignation in now and I'll start booking tickets, then we must pack." "We'll have to tell our parents; they'll get a bit of a shock." "We have mentioned to them that it was on the cards that we would need to move to the States." "Yes, but that was sometime in the future and this is a bit sudden." Elizabeth typed out her resignation citing their immediate move to America, but then Daniel said "I think we should lay another false trail. Say we are moving to South Africa instead. I'm going to organize all of my computer equipment to be packed up and shipped to the states and stored until we are settled. That can all be picked up tomorrow, and then we can be off.

So, Elizabeth altered her resignation letter and emailed it to the personnel officer at the hospital, and went upstairs and started packing. Daniel started looking for flights to America and decided on Chicago, rather than New York. "Why don't we turn this into a holiday as well. I would like to end up on the west coast eventually, San Francisco or Los Angeles, as I would like to try selling the film rights to the game. I would like to have as big a success as Lara Croft Tomb Raider." "It's just because you fancy Angelina Jolie." "And what about your crush on Brad Pitt?" "Ok, truce. Yes, a holiday would be nice." "What about a train journey across America." "I love train journeys, that would be great." So, Daniel investigated rail journeys from Chicago Union Station, and saw there were several long journeys to the southern states or west coast. The one that particularly took his eye was the Amtrak Empire Builder from Chicago to Seattle or Portland. "I've found this one Lizzie, the journey takes 45 hours but you can buy Multi city tickets which means you can get off and stay at one of the stops on the way, and they have First-Class Private Bedroom Suites, with all meals included, and an observation car which has a glass roof." "That sounds amazing Daniel." "There are vacancies on the Empire Builder in a few days' time, but I want to pay cash rather than use my credit card, so I'll wait to book it until were there."

Daniel, realising they would have to use their passports and their names would be on the flight passenger list but not wanting to draw attention to themselves, bought two economy return flights to Chicago on his American Express credit card for Daniel and Elizabeth Seymour, but then bought two single air fare tickets from Heathrow to Johannesburg for each of them on his UK credit card under their real names flying on the previous day. After he had booked the flights Daniel said, "I have a little surprise for you." "What is it?" We are flying from Manchester, so we can visit you parents before we leave." Elizabeth hugged Daniel so tight he could hardly breathe. "Thank you Darling, I wouldn't have liked to have just upped sticks and left without seeing them and saying goodbye" "I didn't think so." "You are so thoughtful Daniel; I think I am the luckiest woman on the planet." "Of course you are" Daniel laughed.

Chapter 52

The following evening, they drove down to East Sussex to say goodbye to Daniel's parents. They all went out for a meal at The

Thatched Inn in Hassocks again, and Elizabeth, who was not drinking alcohol, looked on enviously at the three of them with a bottle of champagne. Goodbyes were said the next morning and they returned to their flat. Daniel went to his office and made sure his computer equipment was securely dismantled, and packed. Along with Daniels computers, they had five large packing cases to be collected by a UPS courier to be sent to America and put into storage until they had found somewhere to live. Locking up their flat, Lizzie handed in the keys to the Letting Agency, who would hopefully find them a suitable tenant, and they boarded a Virgin train from Euston to Manchester Piccadilly. They stayed that night with Elizabeth's family who were delighted to see them and insisted on taking them out for a farewell meal.

It was a huge send off, Tom was recently married and his wife Gillian was expecting a baby, Joe and Robert both brought their girlfriends, Amy and Sarah respectively, but at the moment Alan was unattached and 'playing the field'. With their 11-seater table they virtually took over the nearby small Indian restaurant, their regular family Friday night haunt, and the owner, who was also the chef, came out from the kitchen to wish Daniel and Elizabeth goodbye and a safe journey. Leaving the restaurant, they said their goodbyes to her brothers and their ladies and as they did not have to be at the airport until half past eleven, they enjoyed a full English breakfast which Mam had cooked for them. "I know what aeroplane meals are like, I don't want that baby starving before its born." she said. "What about me?" Daniel asked. "You're big enough and daft enough to look after yourself." She replied laughing. Mam and Dad got in the taxi with them to Manchester airport and at the departure gate more goodbyes were said with Elizabeth and her Mam in tears and Dad wasn't far off either. "We'll see you soon, and send pictures of the baby when he or she makes an entrance," Daniel promised "then you'll have to come over and see us." "I'm sure we'll try," Dad said, Mam being unable to speak.

It was only just after 11 o'clock when Daniel and Elizabeth headed for the check in desk and, remembering to use their Cayman Islands passports, checked in their hold luggage, got their boarding cards and headed for security. They were standing in line to pass through security and noticed a commotion just ahead of them in the line. Two airport security officers were talking to a man just ahead of them in the queue. The man was quite animated, but they couldn't quite make out what was being said. "They are not looking for us, are they? I'm sure Klara recognised me, what if she told her parents and they are now out looking for us?" Elizabeth said, "I shouldn't think so, no one knows where we are or where we're going," Daniel replied, but there was a nervousness in his answer. One of the airport security men picked up a telephone. "Harry, can you come down, we have some concerns with a bag."

A few moments later a man in an airport business suit with a Manchester Airport Group emblem on the top pocket and wearing an airport identification lanyard came down to the security lane. He asked the security man what his concerns were, looked at the x-ray image and then spoke to the passenger. "Sir, can you tell me what is in your case please." "Just open it and have a look." "No sir I am not going to open it until you tell me what is inside." "What is the problem?" "I have concerns about some of the items in your case and until I am satisfied, the case will not be accepted." "Look mate, I'm in a hurry and I might miss my flight." "I'm sorry about that sir, but until I am satisfied about the contents of your case, neither you or the case will proceed beyond this point." "Well just open it then." "As I've already said sir, I am not opening the case until you can satisfy me as to the contents." It was then that several police officers, many carrying guns, walked into the security area. "Daniel, look at the police, and the guns." "I'm sure there's nothing to worry about Lizzie. Just try to stay calm," but Daniel was also worried, and he realised he had called her Lizzie. What if Elizabeth was right. It did look as though they were only concerned about the contents of the case, but what if the police were looking for something, or someone else.

The man was getting quite agitated, "Look mate, I'm going to miss my flight, just open the bloody case will you and see what's in it." "Sir, I'm not your mate, and I have concerns as to what is in your case. If you don't answer my questions and satisfy me as to what is in your case, then the appropriate authority will deal with that." "Aren't you the appropriate authority then." "Only to deal with you at this point sir, now please tell me what is in your case." "I'm not telling you. I've given you permission to open my case, now just get on with it and let me get on my plane." "I'm sorry sir, that case will now be confiscated and I will ask you to come with me." "I'm not going anywhere with you; I'm getting on my flight." Harry signalled to a police officer, who came over and said quietly to the man. "Sir please come with me and do not make a scene." "This pillock will not let me catch my flight." "We will try to sort that out for you sir, now please come with me," took hold of his arm and led him away. Harry then said to the waiting passengers, "I'm sorry about the delay, but this lane will now have to be closed, so please move to the next lane." The lane belts were altered by the security team and they shuffled forward to the next lane. Daniel and Elizabeth looked at each other and she sighed "Guilty conscience?" "I think so, and it is a good job we got here a bit early." Eventually they passed through security and into the departure lounge and boarded the 14:25 Aer Lingus flight to Chicago. There was a 1 hour or so layover at Dublin, but their baggage was transferred to the new plane without them, having to see it again.

Chapter 53

Arriving at O'Hare airport at 19.05, they passed through immigration and took a taxi to the Four Seasons Hotel in East

Delaware Place. It was almost 10 p.m. before they checked in and after being shown to their room, and with the 6-hour time difference making itself felt, they quickly got ready for bed and were almost asleep before their heads touched the pillows. They woke early next morning due to jet lag, breakfasted and had a short walk from the hotel down to the bay, and sat in the sunshine at a coffee shop 'people watching'. They strolled further along the bay promenade and had lunch overlooking the bay, before returning to the hotel, where they had an afternoon nap, something that Elizabeth was finding more necessary with each passing day, showered and changed for dinner in the hotel restaurant. Next morning, they went to the Amtrak booking office at Chicago Union Station and booked a First-Class Private Bedroom Suite, Multi city tickets from Chicago to Seattle, leaving in five days' time.

When their taxi had pulled up outside Union Station and they entered the building, they were awestruck by the magnificence of the architecture. Built in 1925 at a cost of $75 million (about $1 billion at current rates), it is the third busiest station in the USA serving around 140,000 passengers boarding 300 trains every day. The Great Hall is covered by a huge glazed arched roof with statues gracing the many niches and columns some of which are topped with delicate stone carvings. and you could be forgiven if you felt you were in an Italian museum.

They spent four more days exploring Chicago, visiting Grant Park, the 360 Observation Deck, where they had dinner marvelling at the view, The Art Institute of Chicago which Elizabeth loved, and took a boat ride around Chicago with the Chicago Architectural Center. Checking out of their hotel, and again paying by cash, the concierge ordered a taxi to take them back to Chicago Union station. Daniel was very careful not to over or undertip the concierge or at any of the restaurants they had been to. That was something that may be remembered should questions be asked later. They wandered around the station admiring the architecture of the fine building, until it was time for their rail journey. Around 2 o'clock they boarded their train and ordered lunch, with a bottle of champagne and a box of chocolates, although as Elizabeth was pregnant, she only had two small sips of the champagne to celebrate before letting Daniel finish the bottle. She did however, devour most of the chocolates. The train pulled out on time at 3.05 p.m. heading for Minnesota, North Dakota, Montana and Washington State.

They settled into their private room, unpacked their night clothes and toiletries. Lunch was served as they left Union Station and travelled into the Illinois countryside, enjoying the scenery with the trees coming into bloom. Their private room was extremely comfortable, but they also explored the train and finding the other facilities available. The car attendant served their dinner of Tempura Shrimp starters, a Flat Iron Steak for Daniel, Atlantic Salmon for Elizabeth and a dessert of White Chocolate Blueberry Cobbler Cheesecake at 8 p.m. After coffee they relaxed reading books, their eyelids drooping, while Daniel enjoyed a cognac. Elizabeth looked on enviously saying, "as soon as I get rid of this lump, I'm having one of those." Daniel looked up from his book, smiled, had a sip of his brandy and said, "It won't be long now sweetheart, then you can have as many as your heart desires," and raising his glass toasted their future. "The time difference was taking its toll and as soon as the car attendant pulled down their beds, they both got ready for bed and slept soundly, the slight motion of the train aiding their sleep.

The next day they watched the Midwest prairies roll by from the Superliner II sightseer observation lounge, which had curved glass roof windows, and got out to stretch their legs at some of the stops, where there was a 10-minute halt for refuelling or change of drivers. On the second day they travelled towards the west coast and stopped for a stroll on the platform at Leavenworth, home of largest maximum-security prison in the US until it was downgraded to medium security in 2005. "I hope we don't end up in there," Elizabeth said. "Don't worry Elizabeth, were going to be fine." It is also home to Fort Leavenworth which is the US military's maximum-security facility. Further on, they viewed Glacier National Park in Montana from the train. They had wanted to spend a couple of days at one of the lodges, but they didn't open until the end of May. "We can always come back later darling," he said, "It's not surprising seeing the amount of snow about." Then there were the Cascade Mountains as they travelled through Oregon and approached Seattle.

Leaving the Empire Builder in Seattle, Daniel said "You do realise it's a special day today." "No, what is it?" "It's Star Wars Day." "What is that?" "May the fourth be with you." Elizabeth playfully punched his arm, but grinned at him "You are such a nerd." Daniel just smiled. They spent a week vacationing staying at the Four Seasons Hotel in a corner Elliott Bay Suite. They visited Mount Vernon, had dinner at the restaurant on the top of the Space needle and rode the Seattle Great Wheel. Eventually, Daniel said "I think I'd better get back to work, I have some ideas for the next release of the game, and we'd better choose somewhere to live." "I think Los Angeles would be OK don't you." "Fine by me."

They checked out of the hotel the next morning and boarded the Amtrak Coast Starlight train taking 35 hours to reach L.A., again booking a private room and travelling in a Superliner Bedroom Suite. Whilst on board Daniel used his laptop to search for properties on the coast near to L.A. They made a shortlist of potential properties and met a realtor in L.A., looking over several properties on his short list before finally deciding to rent a large airy four bedroomed condo overlooking the bay in Santa Monica where they settled in to await the birth of their baby. The condo was on the top floor of the block and had two large lifts and had parking space for two cars. Something they felt would be necessary with baby strollers etc. "We are going to have to look for cars Daniel." "Yes, I know, I think we'll get one first, more like a people carrier so that we can carry my little bundle of joy around." "Yes, that's fine, but what about the baby?" she laughed. "Yeah, what about it?"

Daniel set himself up in one of the smaller rooms as his software office and got back to developing the next release of his game, while Elizabeth looked at interior decoration magazines and baby clothes catalogues and made plans to redecorate and kit out the nursery.

Chapter 54

Klara was allowed to go home with a clean bill of health, after more tests and rest, two days later. She hadn't rested much though, spending most of her time playing with the other children in the ward in the day room. She was very quiet at home, not the bright happy girl she had been before her accident. Days passed and still Klara did not cheer up. Stephanie was quite worried and said so to Marcus.

Eventually Marcus and Stephanie decided that they should speak to her. Klara was sitting in the lounge reading quietly and they sat down beside her and Marcus said "Klara Liebste, what is the matter, why are you so sad." Klara just shook her head. "You aren't in trouble Klara, it's just that Mummy and Daddy are worried about you. Does your arm still hurt, or your head?" "No, it's not that," Klara wailed and leant against Stephanie, "why doesn't she like me." "Who doesn't like you Liebste." "Izzy." Stephanie gently cuddled her, stroked her head, and said "We explained that to you Klara, Izzy was in an accident and went to live with the angels in heaven." "No, not that Izzy, Izzy in the snow." "Who was that Darling," Stephanie asked. "Izzy in the hospital". "There was no Izzy in the hospital sweetheart." "Yes there was," and Klara burst out crying again. "Why doesn't she like me, she looked after me. I thought she liked me." "When was that darling." "When I was little in the snow." Marcus and Stephanie looked at each other over the top of Klara's head. "What did your Izzy in the snow look like?" "She was nice. And the snowman was nice. We built a real snowman and we said rhymes. I said 'Das ist der Daumen' and the snowman said about the piggy." "What was it about the piggy?" "It went to market, and it tickled." "The snowman said about the piggy." "Yes, he was funny and tickled me." Marcus was confused "The snowman said about the piggy and tickled you." "Yes, well not the real snowman, Izzy's snowman." "What was his name?" "I don't know, he was just the snowman, he was always covered in snow." "Was Izzy pretty?" "Yes, she is, with red hair, you saw her at the hospital." "Was that the lady in the white coat?" "Yes." "Well, she had to go home because she wasn't feeling well, don't you remember, she is having a baby and felt faint. I'm sure it wasn't because she doesn't like you." "I only wanted to say thank you for looking after me, and she can say thank you to the snowman for me." "I'll speak to the hospital and maybe we can go and see her when you get your plaster cast off." "Can we really?" "Yes, of course we can." At that Klara brightened up and stopped crying.

Marcus and Stephanie went into the study while Klara went back to her book. Marcus sat at his desk and on his laptop, he googled 'piggy, market' Wikipedia came up with '*This little piggy went to market.*' "Steph" he said, "It's an English nursery rhyme, look." They both read the nursery rhyme. "It is similar to 'Das ist der Daumen' although not the same," said Stephanie thoughtfully, "Izzy, erm…. Izzy, the doctors name was ..erm… Elizabeth something. Could that be Lizzie?" Marcus searched google again. Elizabeth I Queen of England, Elizabeth II Queen of England. Then he googled Elizabeth name shortened. "That's it," he cried, "it says shortened versions are Libby or Lizzy. And the snowman, do you still have the pictures they sent to us." "Yes of course they are still on my phone." Stephanie opened her phone gallery and there were the pictures sent by the kidnappers of Klara with a snowman. "The snowman, that's what she remembers," said Stephanie "What are you going to do Marcus?" "I'm going to try to find them. I'll get one of my aides to visit the hospital on some pretext and try to find out about this Doctor Lizzie."

Chapter 55

The next morning at the Embassy, Marcus called in his security attaché, Bernhard Remlinger. Bernhard was well over 6 feet tall with blonde hair and blue eyes. He was quite slim and kept fit by regularly using the Embassy gym. "Come in Bernhard," said Marcus following his knock on the door, "I have a little errand for you." He then explained the situation regarding Klara's accident and her wishing to thank the doctor. "Could you go to the hospital for me and find out when the doctor is on duty." "Of course, Mr. Ambassador." Bernhard went to the Chelsea and Westminster Accident Hospital carrying a large bouquet of flowers and in the A&E department asked the receptionist if he could speak to the doctor who had treated his niece, Klara Meir. "She was brought in eight or nine days ago, on Easter Saturday I think, and was kept in for observation for a couple of days." The receptionist looked on the computer and found the case. "The doctor in charge of the case was Dennis Konstantis." "Oh, I thought it was a lady doctor." "Not what it says on my computer." "Is Dr Konstantis on duty." "Not today, but he is working tomorrow. Starts at 7.30 a.m." "Thank you for your help." Bernhard returned to the Embassy where he reported back to Marcus. "That can't be right she was treated by a lady doctor." "I'll go back to the hospital and check with him tomorrow morning Mr. Ambassador." "OK Thank you."

The following morning at 7.35 a.m. Bernhard asked at reception to speak to Dr Konstantis. "I'm sorry sir he is with a number of patients. I will ask him to come and speak to you when he is free. If you would like to wait in the waiting area please." Bernhard sat in the waiting area, and checked his emails on his phone. As time went on and all emails had been dealt with, he opened a game of solitaire. He had got through two cups of watery coffee from the dispensing machine, and several games of solitaire before he heard his name called.

Bernhard stood up and saw a tall bearded man in blue scrubs at the door into the triage unit. "You asked to see me? how can I help you sir," the doctor asked. "Well, my niece Klara Meier was brought in here eight or nine days ago." "Yes, yes, the broken arm, fell off a roundabout as I recall." "Yes that's right, but she seems to think it was a lady doctor who looked after her." "No, no it was me, not a serious fracture I think, should heal quite quickly. Is there a problem?" "Well Klara seems to think it was a lady doctor she saw, and if you forgive me, the beard probably rules that out." They both laughed. "Yes, I agree, oh wait a minute, Yes, I did take over that case from Dr Wells, yes, she felt unwell, she is pregnant and almost fainted I understand, so had to go home, then I took over, but Dr Wells didn't see her for long, only about 10 minutes or so." "Is Dr Wells alright now?" "I couldn't tell you, haven't seen her, well, since then actually, we're a bit like ships that pass in the night, although to be completely accurate, I didn't even see her then, she had already left the hospital and I was messaged to take over and look at Klara. Lovely little girl. I did not have to do much; Dr Wells had organised the x-ray and I just looked at the x-ray and sent Klara off to the fracture room for the plaster cast. Then of course she did have to be admitted because of the potential of a head injury, being unconscious at the time, etc., etc." "Thank you for your help doctor and I hope I haven't disrupted your day too much." "Not at all, hope I can have been of help, and that the arm heals nicely."

Bernhard then returned to reception and asked if he could speak to Dr Wells. "I'm sorry sir, she doesn't work here anymore." "Oh, that seems sudden." "I understand that her husband moved to South Africa and she had to go with him." "Ok, well, you don't have a phone number or forwarding address, do you?" "I'm sure you'll understand sir we are not allowed to give out any staff information." "Yes of course, thank you for your help." Bernhard returned to the Embassy and asked to see the Ambassador. "Sir, it appears that Dr Wells has left the country and has gone to South Africa. Apparently, her husband went and she went with him." "Mmm.... How very strange. See if you can track down what flight they left on could you?" "Yes sir."

Bernhard returned to his office and searched flights from the day of Klara's accident for a Doctor Wells travelling to any of the international airports in South Africa. There were no results. He then took out the title doctor. Still, no one flew to South Africa during that time period. He then had a brainwave. He rang each of the airlines and asked if there were any no shows for flights to South Africa. British Airways came up trumps. There were two no shows, two days after Klara's accident, one was a Daniel Hodge, the other an Elizabeth Wells. He asked to see the Ambassador, but he was in a meeting with the British Home Secretary and not to be disturbed. "Please ask him to call me urgently once his meeting is over," he asked the Ambassadors PA. Just before 5 the PA called Bernhard and told him the Ambassador would see him now. He entered the Ambassadors office and said "Mr Ambassador, there is something fishy going on," and related what he had found out. "Thank you, Bernhard, I'll have to give that some thought."

That night after Klara had finished her homework and gone to bed, Marcus and Stephanie sat in the lounge and considered the information Bernhard had found out. Marcus pondered "Dr Wells sees Klara, almost faints, leaves the hospital, resigns, books a ticket to South Africa, allegedly with her husband, but then they don't board the plane. Very strange behaviour." "What do you think we should do?" "Well, I could ask Bernhard to check all of the flights leaving England, but they could have crossed the channel, back to France, by ferry or Eurostar, could still be in England somewhere. It could be a long search, and I don't think I could justify using the Embassy resources for that. We could hire a private detective, what do you think?" Stephanie was quiet for some time. Marcus could see that she was weighing up the alternatives. "The only thing that is bothering me is that Klara is upset that she thinks the doctor didn't want to see her." Marcus thought for a few moments then "OK, If you think about it, that probably isn't the case. If she is the one that looked after Klara all those years ago, she obviously cared about her. If Klara recognised her, and presumably she recognised Klara, she may well have panicked and thought she could be arrested for kidnapping, end up in prison and lose the ransom money they got, so they have fled, probably the country, to start over somewhere else. I am grateful that we have Klara, and if Cadieux was right, if it hadn't been for them, we wouldn't have her. When we got her back, I was consumed with revenge, and would have done anything to see them punished, but now, seeing Klara as a happy little girl, I am happy to let it rest. Let them get on with their lives and their guilt." "I think I agree with you, I just don't know what to tell Klara. She is very upset, thinking this lady who looked after her doesn't want anything more to do with her." "I know, I don't know what we can do about that." "Let's see if she gets over it." "I might get Bernhard to see if he can dig up something on the husband, there must be marriage records."

Next morning Bernhard was again summoned. "Bernhard, I am going to ask you to do something for me personally, not as the Ambassador and nothing in relation to the German Embassy. If it is something that you are not comfortable doing, please feel free to decline, and nothing more will be said. All I can tell you is that it is not illegal and that you will not be asked to commit a crime, nor will you be asked to something you are not happy with." "Yes Mr Ambassador, what can I help you with." So Marcus, while not telling Bernhard everything, did provide a synopsis of the occurrences of 2005. "So you see my dilemma. Klara would like to speak to this doctor but obviously the doctor may well be afraid of the consequences. I have decided that I will not bring charges against her, after all she, well they, saved my daughter's life, for which I, and my wife, are eternally grateful. It is possible that this Dr Elizabeth Wells is now married and married women change their name to that of their husband. There must be records of her training and her family background. Can you see what you can find out?" "Mr Ambassador that would be a pleasure, and I must say a nice change from the other work I do."

Chapter 56

Bernhard went back to his office and set to work. He carried out a search of the staff at the Chelsea and Westminster Accident Hospital. He was easily able to see the name of Doctor Elizabeth Wells. He found out that she had graduated with honours from Newcastle University in 2009, and had secured a place as a junior doctor at the Chelsea and Westminster hospital the same year. Searching the Newcastle University database and student websites, he ascertained that her family were from Manchester and had four brothers and a sister. He searched census records from 1991 and 2001 and discovered that she had lived with her parents until leaving for university. The University records showed that she had lived in student accommodation until 2004 when she had moved into private accommodation in Middlesbrough.

He reported this back to Marcus and asked if he should visit her family in Manchester. "I think that would be a good idea," Marcus replied. The next morning Bernhard climbed into his car and set off for Manchester. He found the family home quite easily and knocked on the door of the terraced house. The house was well maintained and in a pleasant working-class area of the city. A lady opened the door wearing an apron and dusting her hands. "Good morning, Mrs Wells, is it?" he said "I'm trying to trace a Doctor Elizabeth Wells, do you know where I can find her?" What do you want with her?" "Well, she looked after a little girl who wants to say thank you, and she has left the hospital and seems to have disappeared." "I'm sorry I can't help you." and closed the front door. "Mmm..." he thought. "Strange. I need to stick around." He phoned Marcus and told him of the response and what he intended to do. "Sounds like a good idea," Marcus responded.

So, Bernhard sat in his car and waited, and waited, and waited, played more solitaire, but also this time he had downloaded a book onto his phone and started reading that. At half past four the front door opened and the lady with her hat and coat on left the house and walked to the end of the street and disappeared around the corner, and Bernhard waited, and waited. Just before quarter to six a car pulled up and a large young man got out, took a key out of his pocket and opened the front door, locked the car, and went in. A little while later a white van pulled up behind the car. 'RW Builders painted on the side.' Another large young man got out of the van, took a key out of his pocket and went inside. Bernhard waited. An older man wearing a donkey jacket and a flat cap walked down the street and let himself into the house.

Just after half past seven, the three men left the house and started walking down the street. Bernhard left his car and followed them at a discreet distance. They walked around the corner and disappeared into the Old Bell pub. He waited a few minutes, then followed them into the pub and saw them at a table with some other men and pints of beer and lager were brought from the bar.

Bernhard found a seat at the bar and ordered a pint of lager. He still hadn't developed a taste for English beer, but the lager wasn't bad. Over the course of the evening, he watched the three men putting the world to rights, quaffing more pints and of course visiting the gents. The older man left around 9.30, "See you tomorrow boys," and left the two younger men sat at the table, now on their own.

Bernhard wandered over and said "Do you mind If I sit here?" "No, it's a free country mate," said one. Bernhard quietly sipped his second lager of the night and eventually one of the two men said. "You don't sound English mate, where you from?" "I'm just visiting from Germany." "Bloody Germans, too good at penalties." Bernhard laughed, "yes but in 1966, They think it's all over, it is now!" That broke the ice. The famous expression from Kenneth Wolstenholme in the World Cup final when Geoff Hurst scored the fourth goal to win the cup for England is etched on every delighted England, and some disappointed German, football supporter's memory and even some who aren't football supporters. Then, the beers flowed and football discussion raged across the table. Who were the best, Manchester United? Bayern Munich? Liverpool? Borussia Dortmund? Arsenal? Nah, Real Madrid, now that IS a team. Then dropping it into the conversation, "Isn't your sister a doctor?" "Yeah, Lizzie, she was down in London." "Has she left then?" "Yeah, gone to the States hasn't she." "On her own then?" "Nah, with her old man Daniel, doin alright as I hear." "Shaddup bruv." "What?" "I said shaddup bruv." "OK, OK, sorry mate, speakin outta turn." "No problem I was only asking. One for the road?" Buying another round of drinks, Bernhard left the pub with a satisfying smile on his face.

Bernhard found an hotel and checked in for the night, leaving early next morning. In his office he searched for marriage records from 2005 for an Elizabeth Wells who had married a Daniel, and there it was in 2009 to a Daniel Hodge. Further investigation showed that a Daniel Hodge had been a computer undergraduate at Teesside University from 2003 to 2006. His parents were successful lawyers living in East Sussex. The census showed their address. Next port of call.

Bernhard drove down to East Sussex the next morning. He drove up to the house which was a large detached period property in its own grounds of about an acre and a half with well-maintained gardens. He parked in front of the house next to a Lexus convertible. Bernhard walked up to the front door and rang the bell. An attractive lady dressed in a cream blouse and charcoal gray trousers answered the door. "Excuse me madam, is it Mrs Hodge?" "Yes, can I help you?" "I'm actually looking for Daniel. I've heard he does some computer programming and I am looking for someone to help me." "Oh, I'm afraid he won't be able to do that he is snowed under with his own company." And which company is that?" "I am afraid I don't keep up with all of that, I'm too into my garden as you can see." "Yes, it looks lovely, well thank you anyway, give him my regards won't you." "And you are?" "My name is Bernhard, but he probably won't remember me."

That night Abigail Hodge phoned her son. "Daniel, do you know a Bernhard?" "Not that I recall mum no." "He said you probably won't remember him, tall chap, blond, probably German from his accent." "No never heard of him." "How is Elizabeth?" "She is fine, mum. Looking forward to the next three weeks, then hopefully it will be all over We are thinking of coming over in a few months' time, after the baby is born and is old enough to travel, but I'm sure both you, dad and Elizabeth's mum and dad will want to come over here before then. Could we stay with you for a week or so?" "Of course dear, you know you are always welcome and we would love to come over and see the baby when he or she arrives. Elizabeth must be getting a bit tired of waiting by now." "Yes, she can be a little frustrated, but we are so looking forward to the birth." "Have you picked out names yet?" "We have a couple of ideas, but as we decided not to know if it's a boy or a girl, we are still on tenterhooks." "Give our love to Elizabeth won't you," "Will do, love to dad, bye"

"So" thought Bernhard to himself "he has his own company. I'll check Companies House." Returning to London Bernhard checked Companies House, but there was no trace of a Daniel Hodge as a director of a company. Again, he reported his findings to Marcus. "Looks like we've hit a dead-end Bernhard, let me think about that for a couple of days and I'll decide what to do next." "Very good Mr. Ambassador." That night he told Stephanie of the progress that Bernhard had made. "I think Daniel is a very clever chap and he has laid a number of false trails. I'm not sure what to do next. He probably formed his company offshore with the banking probably there as well." "Don't get yourself upset about it. We've got Klara back and that's all that matters." "How is Klara? is she alright about the lady doctor?" "She seems fine and hasn't mentioned her in the last couple of days. Maybe we can just let it go." "Yes maybe."

Chapter 57.

Summer 2011, or what passed for summer, was disappointing in many ways, but in fact records show that only 2006 was warmer for 353 years since records began. Gravesend recorded 33.1° C, the hottest in the UK for five years. It was early July and Bernhard and his new girlfriend, Melanie, who worked in a travel agency, were sitting at an outside table enjoying a pub lunch, and he asked her "In the travel business, are there ways of tracking passengers who were no shows?" "Yes, it can be done, why, what's the problem?" "It's just something that's been niggling me. My boss asked me a couple of weeks ago if I could find out about someone. They had booked a flight to Johannesburg but then did not show up." "Did they get a refund?" "I don't know." "Maybe they changed their minds and went somewhere else." "Possibly, but that is like trying to find a needle in a haystack." "I suppose you know their names." "Yes, but from what I could see they didn't fly anywhere else from Heathrow." "We have a link to airlines at the office, I could look at it for you." "Would you, that would be great."

That afternoon Melanie sat at her computer, and while it was quiet, she searched all airlines for the names of Daniel Hodge and Elizabeth Wells travelling between 25th April and the 10th May. There were no results. She rang Bernhard "Have you got their dates of birth?" "I'll look them up and text them to you." A few minutes later Melanie's phoned pinged with a new text message *Daniel Hodge, born Haywards Heath 17th May 1983, Elizabeth Wells born Manchester 28th October 1985*. Melanie thought hard. She did a search on dates of birth. There were over 30 hits of people who were born on those dates, and two of the dates had travelled together, Daniel and Elizabeth SEYMOUR." She rang Bernhard and passed on the information. "That, my clever little girl, earns you a very fine dinner." "I was thinking more of a romantic weekend, maybe even Paris." "You're on."

Bernhard then did some research and three days later went to see Marcus. "Mr. Ambassador," Bernhard said when shown into the office, "I might have discovered something about your missing people." "Go on." "A Daniel and Elizabeth Seymour with the same dates and places of birth for Daniel Hodge and Elizabeth Wells flew from Manchester Airport to Chicago O'Hare airport, the day after Hodge and Wells did not show up for their flight to South Africa. They travelled on Cayman Islands passports issued in 2008. There is a Daniel Seymour and Elizabeth Seymour who are directors of a holding company in the Cayman Islands that have three subsidiary companies writing and selling computer gaming software. The companies are doing quite well. I have not yet located their address as the corporate address is a lawyer's office in the Caymans." "That is excellent work Bernhard." "I can't take all of the credit sir, my girlfriend Melanie is a travel agent, and she found out the travel information. Once I had that it is just trying to follow their trail. At the moment I am at a dead end in Chicago, but I wanted to know if you would like me to dig a little further or let it go." "I'll mull it over tonight and let you know tomorrow, but well done, and of course to Melanie." "Thank you, sir."

Later that evening after dinner and Klara was in bed, Marcus told Stephanie what Bernhard had found out. Stephanie said "So, they've changed their names, now have Cayman Islands passports and have a successful company." "Yes, that's about the size of it, but do we bring it all crashing down around them?" "Could we not just get the money back?" "Well, we could try, I could pass this on to Cadieux of course. I'm sure he would be only too happy to chase it up and put them behind bars." Stephanie was thoughtful for a little while, then "Marcus, I really do not want to do that. They saved our little girls life and I do not want them to end up in prison. Remember your speech to the French police. I'm not even really bothered about the money; I am fortunate to have enough, we are fortunate to have enough. I would just like them to meet Klara again, and I would like to thank them." "Okay, I don't disagree with anything you've said, and I do remember my speech and I meant every word of it. I'll ask Bernhard to try to trace them and let's see where that goes, and see if we can let Klara meet them Eh?"

Next morning Marcus called Bernhard into his office. "Bernhard, that was excellent work. What I want you to do is now take unpaid leave from the Embassy, which I will approve. I will pay you personally for your time and expenses, as it really shouldn't be on the German taxpayer. I would like you to try to locate the Seymour's without their knowledge and hopefully provide contact details and addresses. Take as much time as you need and if you need to travel abroad, that is also fine by me, and take Melanie with you if you want." "Thank you, Mr. Ambassador." "No Bernhard, thank you and I will also explain fully why I'm looking for them, because I think it's right that you have the full story." Marcus then gave Bernhard the full details of everything that had happened in France. Bernhard stood up to take his leave and said "Mr. Ambassador, I appreciate your candour and I will do my best to locate them for you."

Bernhard took his unpaid leave and working from his flat started his search. He went back to 2005 and checked crossings to France over the ferry system, nothing. Then surprisingly with Eurotunnel, he hit lucky. "Got him," he exclaimed and telephoned the Ambassador. "Yes Bernhard, have you found anything?" "Yes Mr. Ambassador, Daniel Hodge and Elizabeth Wells left England for France in a VW camper van buy Eurostar at 6.05 a.m. on Sunday 13th February 2005, returning on Wednesday 2nd March at 17.25. This ties in with the period you are looking for and that pretty much ties them in as well." "So, they were in France when the accident happened and they left the day after the ransom was paid. That seems like a coincidence, a very big coincidence I think, and I do not believe in coincidences. What do you want to do now Bernhard?" "I thought I might go to Chicago if that's ok sir." "By all means Bernhard, and take Melanie if she's free. I'll transfer £5000 now to your account and text me if you need more." "Thank you, sir, I'll bring back the receipts." "Don't bother Bernhard, take it as a bonus. You've done well."

Chapter 58

Bernhard took Melanie out for dinner that night and when they were drinking their coffee, he sprang his surprise. "You said you would like a romantic weekend, maybe in Paris." Her eyes lit up, "Yes" "How about Chicago instead?" "Do you mean it, what for a weekend?" "Certainly, but it will be more than a weekend. I'm going, it's just up to you if you're coming with me. It could take some time." "I'll speak to my boss and get some time off." Having been granted leave of absence from the travel agency, she met Bernhard at his flat where they checked all of the flights departing Chicago O'Hare for the next month, but no Seymour's. Where can they have gone, he thought, Maybe the Cayman Islands. He checked all known airlines with flights to the Cayman Islands, again no Seymour's. "I suppose it's obvious that he used his credit card flying to Chicago, I mean they would have had to use passports so no way of hiding that, but once they're in the States, well cash is king." Melanie said. "Melanie, I think you've hit the nail on the head again. When we get to Chicago, we'll just have to try to think like him, or them."

Four days later they flew from Heathrow to Chicago. When they stepped out from O'Hare airport, they discovered the first obstacle, taxis. Hundreds of them it seemed. Lined up ready to take the arrivals anywhere. "It's no use trying the taxi drivers, they wouldn't remember a couple from some weeks ago. We'll think about this more at the hotel." They checked into a hotel went to the restaurant for dinner, then let the jet lag catch up and slept until they both woke early. "Might be only 5 o'clock here, but it's eleven in London. But I'm wide awake now, how about you Melanie." "Yes, I'm fine. Now we need to try to find a needle in the Chicago haystack."

They started out before breakfast, brainstorming, but made coffee from the supply in their room. "If you were running away, and didn't want to be found, what would you do?" he asked Melanie. "Not that I've had to do that before, but obviously try to cover my tracks, use different forms of transport, use cash, not credit cards wherever possible." "Right, you've landed in Chicago, probably jetlagged, like we were, booked into a hotel, and if you're right, used cash. From here, what do you do, where do you go. You have plenty of money. What is the simplest and easiest way to hide where you're going, fly, hire a car, take a train, take a bus?" "I don't think they would have flown, too easy to track." "Agreed, and there must be hundreds of car hire places in Chicago, if not more. I would avoid the big names like Hertz, Alamo and Enterprise, who would want identification, and pick a small outfit, but that could take weeks." "Let's look at buses and trains first." "There's Greyhound and Amtrak, they are the biggest. We know they landed on the 26th April. They may not have left straight away but probably, what? within a week say. You check Greyhound, I'll do Amtrak."

So, Melanie started with Greyhound, but soon found that this was going to be impossible. The number of routes leaving Chicago was enormous and a large percentage of travellers bought their tickets in cash. "Sorry Bernhard, this isn't going to be feasible, there's just too much to check and too many imponderables." "OK Melanie, help me with Amtrak. There are a lot of trains but not as many as buses." They opened the Amtrak website and downloaded the map and set up a spreadsheet with all of the destinations of the long-distance trains, their thinking being that anyone fleeing would try to hide away as far as possible from their last known location. There were obviously four directions that could be taken, nothing went North into Canada, except north east into Montreal, which was a possibility to then change trains to Canadian Pacific. "We'll put that on the back burner for now," decided Bernhard. There was East to the Eastern seaboard from Maine down to Florida and including New York, South to Georgia across to Texas and Arizona, and West to Seattle down to Los Angeles. "Where would they go to get lost," he mused. "Or where would she want to go, probably somewhere warm. I know I would." "Right, let's leave the East coast northern section, but think of Florida across to Texas, and California to Arizona."

They searched everything they could think of, but found nothing. "They could have stopped off in Oklahoma or Colorado or even Las Vegas." "Bernhard, they could have stopped off anywhere." "True." "I wonder if a Private Investigator would help." "It couldn't hurt." So, Bernhard looked online and found a number of Private Investigator Agencies listed. Some had reviews and he found one that seemed to be well thought of, so he dialled the number. A lady answered the phone "Ronnie's Agency, how can ah help." "Is Ronnie available please?" "Yes I am." "I'm sorry, I just expected a man." "Don't worry the next time someone expects a woman will be the first." Bernhard explained what he was trying to do and would Ronnie be able to help. "Can you come to my office tomorrow morning at 11 and bring whatever information you have. My charges are $350 a day plus." "Plus?" "Expenses." "Yes of course, right I'll see you tomorrow."

Chapter 59.

At 11 the next morning Bernhard and Melanie sat outside Ronnie's office in downtown Chicago. I wasn't in the most salubrious of districts, but neither was it rundown. They were met by a middle-aged African American lady with grey starting to show in her short dark hair, and shown into a comfortable office which had stacks of boxes on the floor and a desk covered in files. "Have you always been a Private Investigator Miss,...... er?" "Just call me Ronnie, everyone does, No I was a Chicago cop for twenty-five years, mainly working missing persons. Found a bunch of 'em. Retired four years ago, got bored, set up on mah own. What is it you want me to do for y'all." Bernhard recounted the story, well most of it, but leaving out the ransom, mainly sticking to the accident and Klara wanting to meet the nice lady doctor. Ronnie listened patiently and when Bernhard finished, she said, "Sorry cain't help yuh." "Why is that?" "Well, you ain't told me the truth boy." "Miss Ronnie, I assure you I have not told you a single lie," "Maybe, maybe not, but there's more to it than that. I cain't see y'all comin' over from England just so's a little girl can say thank yuh to some lady doctor." Bernhard was impressed by Ronnie's insight and realised if he wanted her help, he would have to tell here everything. "No, Ronnie, you're right. That is the main reason why we're here, but it isn't everything." So, Bernhard told Ronnie the full story. "OK," she said "Nows I'll help y'all. You're in luck, on two counts. One, finished a case yesterday. Two, know some people with both Amtrak and Greyhound. Long distance you think? two young people, paying cash, English, lady pregnant, not that frequent, Ah'll see what ah kin find." And Bernhard and Melanie left Ronnie to start her search.

They also continued looking at the map and destinations trying to come up with a result, but two days later, Ronnie rang. "Got some news for y'all. Young couple, likely English, she was pregnant it seems, got on the Empire Builder on May 2nd travelling to Seattle. Got there May 4th." "Mmm....Star Wars Day," Bernhard said quietly. "Ah heard y'all, Star Wars fan are yuh." "'Fraid so," he replied, "That's a great step forward. It gives me something to look at anyway." "Ah don't think ah kin be of any more help if they's on the west coast, don't like leavin' Chicago, might get lost. See if I can get you a number though and text it through. I'll send ma bill." "Thanks, Ronnie, for all your help." "Don't mention it." "Looks like we're going to Seattle Melanie."

Chapter 60

Bernhard and Melanie didn't waste time with the Empire Builder, but flew to Seattle the next day. Ronnie had sent a text with another P.I's name and number. After they had landed, they called and this time it was a man who answered. Bernhard introduced himself and Tyrell said "I've been expecting you, Ronnie phoned and said you might call. Come by and see me tomorrow anytime," and gave his address.

Next morning Bernhard and Melanie rang the bell at Tyrells office door. Now Bernhard was tall but slim, Tyrell was African American and huge. He must have been 6 feet 8 and big with it. Not fat, no, certainly not fat. He had muscle where neither Bernhard or Melanie thought muscle should be. His voice however belied his stature. It was soft and gentle. "Come on in." he invited, and they followed him into an amazing office. It was like walking onto a sci-fi film set. There were three desks with at least two large computer screens on them and a huge TV screen fixed to the wall. An attractive lady was busy at one of the computers. Tyrell introduced her, "This is my wife Chantal and the brains behind the business." "Nice to meet you." Both Bernhard and Melanie said. Chantal smiled "Likewise, can I get you coffee?" "That would be lovely, no cream for me please," said Melanie. "I'll get it Chantal," and Tyrell went through to a small kitchen and brought out four cups on a tray and a plate of cookies, which he set down on a low table beside four huge easy chairs. Chantal joined them and they all sat. "Now then," started Tyrell, "after your call yesterday, I spoke with Ronnie and she filled me in on your problem and as I understand it you only want to locate them and provide contact details for Mr Meier." "Yes, that's right." "Now just to make it clear from my side, you don't wish to do any harm to this couple," "No certainly not. Mr & Mrs Meier are most grateful to the Seymour's as they are now known, for saving their little girls life." "Yes but 400 grand, that's a lot of dough." "I know, but they are very wealthy and Mr Meier is the German Ambassador to London, so it would not go down too well in the press if he ordered a hit now would it." "No, I s'pose not. Not like American politics then," and chuckled. "Ok then our fees are $500 per day plus." "Expenses right." "That's right and we take $1000 up front. We are state of the art in here, and we are pretty good at what we do, even if I say so myself, I wouldn't expect it to take too long. Chantal here will start immediately we get your funds." "Give me your bank details and I'll transfer the funds now." The transaction completed they left Tyrell and Chantal to get on with the search.

They returned to their hotel and as they entered their room Bernhards phone rang. It was Tyrell. "They are not in Seattle; they took the Coast Starlight train on May 12th which arrived in L.A. on the 14th. Sorry can't help in L.A. don't have a licence to operate there, we'll reimburse you $500. Didn't spend no expenses, so just the minimum of one day." "Tyrell, you said you were good, but I didn't expect that good, I must say that's pretty impressive." "Hope you find them. Don't have no contacts in L.A. though," and hung up. "Melanie, were off to L.A.," and phoned Marcus to tell him the news. Marcus was delighted at the progress and approved of the hiring of the private investigators.

Chapter 61

Bernhard and Melanie now flew into LAX, Los Angeles International Airport. They checked into a hotel, but were now on their own. Neither Ronnie or Tyrell had been able to give any advice, help or contacts. They looked online for private investigators and checked out three, but were unhappy about either the person themselves or the fee they charged. "I suppose it's because its L.A.," Melanie said "All this money around." "If they're in L.A. they must be living somewhere, what about checking with house rentals." "Could be a good idea Bernhard. Let's get the spreadsheets out again and start work." "If they have all of this money available, I'm sure they would want to live in a nice area in a nice house or condo." "Let's start there and see where we end up." So, they created a new spreadsheet and every day they sat at the table in their hotel room, and called realtors. "At least we're looking for a pregnant lady," said Bernhard "Not if she's had the baby." "Melanie, why didn't I think of that," "Because you're not a woman." "Let's check the hospitals for a baby Seymour." That was easier said than done.

Hospitals weren't in the habit of giving out personal information. No matter how they tried, they couldn't locate baby Seymour. They went back to calling realtors with the same disappointing result.

Daniel's software game was selling well, and the company were making big profits. He was working hard on the next version, but was convinced that the game could be transported to the big screen and was still making phone calls, going to meetings in L.A. and Hollywood trying to sell the film rights, but to date no one would listen or better still but the rights. This week he had meetings scheduled with three studios. While he was out, Elizabeth was at home looking after their daughter Claire. Elizabeth was still in the first flush of motherhood and enjoying every sleepless moment of it. She was sure soon the overwhelming tiredness would kick in and she and Daniel, who to be fair was helping in every way he could, except for the breast feeding of course, would end up like zombies from lack of sleep. But in the meantime, she felt like she was walking on air. She was sitting in her favourite chair, Claire asleep in her arms her little face puckered up as most babies are and Elizabeth took one of Claire's little hands and recited
"Das ist der Daumen
der schüttelt die Pflaumen,
der hebt sie auf,
der trägt sie nach Haus,
und der Kliene isst sie alle auf."

Then the door to the condo burst open and Daniel rushed into the room, ran over to Elizabeth picked them up in his arms and cuddled them gently to him "I've done it, I've sold the film rights to my game," he whispered, beaming. "How much for." "$950,000. I had offers from two studios and that was the best offer." Elizabeth put Claire down into her cot, flung her arms around her husband and kissed him. "You are amazing. I love you. But why $950,000 and not a million?" "I suppose they just wanted to show they were negotiating. I did push for the million, but they wouldn't budge, however I did get them to add 5% of the profits. I couldn't have done it without you. Now we can start planning for our expansion. But I have had an idea which I think you'll like."

Chapter 62

Gerry was bursting. If his pride was any greater, he would surely explode. He was dressed in a new suit, crisp cream shirt and his UPS tie. Today he was not a UPS delivery driver. He was not even a UPS assistant manager, today he was the Domestic Delivery Manager of the Kentish Town UPS depot. Madeline was not working today and she smiled at him from their bed, "You look very handsome Darling, and business like too." He leant over the bed and kissed his wife, "I hope to be back around 3 this afternoon, have a nice day," "You too," she replied "Love you." and he set off for his 10-minute walk to the Regis Road depot.

Gerry had been promoted to assistant manager at the Lyon depot four years ago and had been highly regarded in that role. Madeline, after completing her journalism course with distinction at the Universite de Lyon, had been working as a local reporter in Lyon at Le Progrès, reporting primarily on local news in the Rhône-Alpes region. Looking to advance her career, she had applied for, and was appointed, as a reporter at The Observer, the world's oldest Sunday newspaper, in England. Gerry had applied for a transfer to a London depot and an assistant delivery manager vacancy was available at the Kentish Town depot and his transfer was approved. Gerry and Madeline married before they left France and were renting a flat in Malden Road, Kentish Town, just a 15-minute walk from the depot and a 10-minute walk for Madeline from Chalk Farm tube station.

This morning was Gerry's first day as manager. He and Madeline had attended the retirement party last night for his boss, Ernest

Gray, at a local pub where the upstairs room has been booked and he and Madeline with help from a couple of drivers had decorated the room with balloons and banners. The area manager had also come along and presented Ernest with a carriage clock in recognition of 25 years with UPS, and the members of the depot had clubbed together and, as he was a keen golfer, bought him a new driver, which they thought was quite appropriate. In his little speech afterwards, he said" I think this driver will go further than some of you lot." Which caused quite a big laugh. Well, a few drinks had been taken, and they were being polite. Gerry only had a couple of drinks so that he would be fine for his first day. Ernest took him to one side and told him he was a fine assistant manager and was sure he would cope with the additional responsibility. Gerry and Madeline left early and walked back to their flat and turned in early as Gerry was getting up for work at 4 a.m.

Arriving at the Regis Road Depot at 5 o'clock, Gerry checked over the deliveries with the drivers and one by one the vans departed. It was approaching 7.15 when he looked out of his office and saw one van was still in the yard. He checked the rotas and found that one driver, Charlie Forbes, had not signed in for work this morning. He rang Charlie's mobile but it went through to voicemail. Gerry left a message asking Charlie to contact him as a matter of urgency. Just what I needed on my first day in charge, thought Gerry. If he doesn't turn up, I'll have to take the van out myself. So, taking off his new jacket and pulling on a UPS issue sweater, he checked the route and the van deliveries. By the time he had finished Charlie still had not returned his call, so Gerry started the van and drove out onto the round. He phoned Madeline and told her he wouldn't be home at 3 o'clock as he hoped, but that when he got home, they would go out for a celebratory meal.

It was a lovely summer day, and to be honest, Gerry was enjoying being back in a van and not at a desk, something he had missed for quite a while. It was almost 5.30 by the time he was delivering his last parcel. It was a large box which was wrapped in clear parcel wrap and through the wrapping he could see a red ribbon around the box and a big red bow with 'Happy Birthday Klara with love' written on the front. He pulled in front of the large house in Phillimore Place and went to the back of the van to get the parcel. He was quite surprised as to how heavy it was. Someone's getting a nice birthday present he thought. He carried the parcel up the front steps and rang the bell. The door was opened by an excited little girl and Gerry said "Delivery for Miss Klara Meier." "That's me," the little girl said, "I'm Klara Meier. Could you bring that into the lounge please." Gerry smiled "Certainly Miss Meier," an carried the parcel into the lounge and set it on the coffee table. "Mummy there's another birthday present for me, come and see," and Stephanie came from the kitchen. "Would you sign for you parcel please Miss?" and handed Klara a pen with his clipboard. Klara carefully signed the delivery receipt. "And a very happy birthday Miss Meier." Gerry was smiling as he left the house thinking what an amazing way to finish his first day as manager. As Gerry walked back to the van a tall blond man got out of a chauffeur driven car and passed him on the steps. "I think there is a very happy little girl inside," he said as he passed. "Yes, said the tall man, it's my daughters 9th birthday today," opened the front door and entered his house.

Chapter 63

It was a perfect day for a nine-year-olds birthday party. A warm and sunny July summers day. The garden at Phillimore Place had been decked out with balloons and banners. Stephanie had arranged for caterers to supply and serve the food, and trestle tables had been erected and food was being loaded onto crisp white tablecloths. The children were having a great time running around in the sunshine. They had been into Holland Park earlier in the afternoon, and rather than tire them out as Stephanie had hoped, it had seemed to give them more energy.

More games were played, then she called the children to come and eat, and the devouring started. Copious quantities of soft drinks were consumed and then the birthday cake was brought out, lit with 9 candles, and Klara did the honours, blowing out the candles in one breath, and then cutting through the chocolate icing. All of the birthday presents were then brought out for Klara to open. Eventually parents called to collect their children, and they left complete with goody bags. The caterers cleared the tables and the debris. Soon the garden was back to its pristine best, well, almost.

Stephanie and Klara snuggled up together on the sofa in the lounge and waited for Marcus to return home. Klara yawned and cuddled in to her mother. There was a ring at the door and Klara leapt up and ran to answer it. There was a man in a uniform holding a parcel tied in a ribbon, with a big red bow and gift label attached reading 'Happy Birthday Klara' on it. "Could you bring it through to the lounge please," Klara asked the man "Mummy there's another birthday present for me, come and see." Klara signed the delivery receipt and said "Can I open it Mummy?" Just then Marcus walked through the front door. Klara ran over and was swamped in his big hug. "Happy birthday sweetheart. Did you just get another present? I saw the van driver delivering it." "Yes Daddy look what has arrived for me." The label on the box said "Happy Birthday Klara, with love."

Stephanie and Marcus leant over watching Klara. She pulled the ribbon off, and lifted the lid. They could not believe their eyes. In the box were three pictures, but it was what was underneath the pictures that was mind boggling. Dollars, loads of them. $100 bills. Neatly stacked into the box. They took out the three pictures, all of a little girl about two or three years old, one asleep into a woman's arms, although her face could not be seen in the picture, another smiling, standing by a snowman with a woolly hat and a carrot nose, and the third, laughing, having a snowball fight with a man who had his back to the camera. Klara looked up at her parents, tears in her eyes and said "That's me isn't it." "Yes darling, that is you, and the people who took you." Marcus growled. "And what's this?" she asked. They counted the money. $500,000.

They couldn't understand it, but then Klara saw something strapped to the underside of the box lid. It was a letter addressed to Klara. She opened it and read it out loud.

Sweet little Klara, how we miss you, now you are back with your Mummy and Daddy, where you should be. You were only with us a short while, but we will never forget those few happy days. You were so special. We are truly sorry for the hurt we caused to your parents, and they may never understand or forgive us, but at least we are able to return what is rightfully yours, and theirs. When we found you in the car, with Alek and Izzy, they were both dead from the crash, and we thought they were your parents. We weren't sure we could save you. You were so cold and probably would not have survived left in the car. We carried you back to our camper van in a snowstorm and then we were snowed in, trapped for days. An opportunity came our way and we took advantage. The newspapers said the police were looking for kidnappers and that gave us the idea. We should not have done so, and can only apologise, to you and your parents, however, you are alive and well, a beautiful little girl, and we hope you have a wonderful life ahead of you.

"Das ist der Daumen
der schüttelt die Pflaumen,
der hebt sie auf,
der trägt sie nach Haus,
und der Kliene isst sie alle auf."

With all our love
Xxx

Marcus sent a text to Bernhard "Come home Bernhard, well done. Its sorted."

Chapter 64

Friday 18th November 2011.
At the BBC Television Centre at the top of Regents Street in London the Children in Need special hosted by Sir Terry Wogan, as he had done since its inception in 1980, was in full swing. Daniel and Elizabeth had settled down to watch. Baby Claire was asleep in her cot and the baby alarm was on the coffee table beside them. They were always amazed at the different things people did to raise money for disadvantaged children, and over the years had contributed almost £1 billion. BBC newsreaders performed a Strictly Come Dancing routine, Gareth Malone had a Children in Need choir, the cast of EastEnders did a Queen medley, there were performances from JLS, One Direction and a super group including Ed Sheeran. It was getting late in London, although only just after 5 p.m. in L.A. when Terry said he had a special guest. He introduced a family of father, mother and their 9-year-old daughter. Sir Terry asked the father to tell his story.

He spoke with a voice full of emotion and a slight German accent. "Some time ago, we lost our daughter." He looked across at the little girl and smiled. She smiled back and he continued, "Our only child was in need, and two young people saved her life and returned her to us. They don't know this, but I know who they are, and what they did. I have a cheque for $500,000 US dollars, I think it is about £325,000 sterling, for Children in Need, to say thank you to those two wonderful people. My wife and I are very grateful for what they did, and they will always be honoured guests in our home." Stephanie took Marcus' hand squeezed it and smiled at him. Sir Terry turned to the little girl and said, "and what is your name?" "I'm Klara." "Klara, would you like to say something?" Klara looked into the camera smiled, started playing with her fingers and spoke

"For Izzy and the snowman"

"Das ist der Daumen
der schüttelt die Pflaumen,
der hebt sie auf,
der trägt sie nach Haus,
und der Kliene isst sie alle auf."

Daniel and Elizabeth looked at Marcus, Stephanie and Klara on the TV, hugged each other and wept with relief. "It's finally over." Elizabeth said.

Chapter 65

It was the week running up to Christmas with snow on the ground and travel in chaos throughout the UK. Houses were decked with lights and decorations. Christmas trees in almost every window and Phillimore Place was no exception. Marcus had been out and bought a huge Christmas tree which had pride of place in the lounge window. Coloured lights were twinkling and baubles hanging all over the tree and tinsel draped across, catching the lights as they sparkled. The room was hung with streamers and glittering decorations. Stephanie and Klara had made a few of the decorations, something Klara insisted upon having been taught how to do it at school. A taxi pulled up outside and a couple got out. The man was wearing a baby carrier with a small baby safely tucked up inside against the weather, and carrying a holdall full of baby things. They carefully walked up the steps which had been cleared of snow and stood apprehensively at the front door. They looked nervously at each other, then Daniel said "Go on Elizabeth, ring the bell."

The bell was rung, and the door opened by a lady with a little girl standing a little behind her. Elizabeth looked down at the little girl and said "Hello Klara, its Lizzie and Daniel and we've brought our baby Claire to see you." Klara ran round from behind her mother and flung her arms around Lizzie, hugged her and cried out with joy. Stephanie smiled and said "Come on in out of the cold and let me see your little one." They went into the hall where Daniel was able to rid himself of the baby carrier, once Claire had been handed over to Stephanie. Marcus came from his study, "What's all the noise about?" "Daddy, it's Lizzie and the snowman, and they've brought Claire." "We named her after Klara sir" said Daniel, "and we must apologise for all the hurt we caused you." Marcus came over to Daniel, towering over him, Daniel stepped back, but Marcus grabbed his hand and pulled him into a bear hug, tears falling down his face. "Nonsense Daniel, you gave us the greatest gift you could, our child." And they all stood in the hall crying, all except Claire who was happily gurgling away in Stephanie's arms. "Mummy can I hold her please?" They went into the lounge and Klara sat, Claire was placed on her lap and Klara took one of Claire's little hands and spoke

"Das ist der Daumen
der schüttelt die Pflaumen,
der hebt sie auf,
der trägt sie nach Haus,
und der Kliene isst sie alle auf."
Everyone laughed.

Chapter 66

It was Sunday morning, and Daniel was drinking coffee and looking through a Beautiful Homes book. They had moved back from Los Angeles and were staying with Daniels parents until they could find a suitable house. Daniel was busy developing his software and was also acting as a consultant on the film of his game. Elizabeth had written to the Chelsea and Westminster hospital and had applied to re-join the junior doctor staff now that Claire was 9 months old. Elizabeth's parents were now rattling around in their house, all their children having flown the nest. Tom and Gillian had bought a nice semi in Rochdale, Joe and Robert had moved into their girlfriends flats, both in Stretford, and Alan was in a flat of his own in Oldham, working for brother Robert's building firm, trying to go straight after his release from prison. Both sets of parents had been overjoyed at seeing their first grandchild, although now there were another two on the way, with both Tom and Joe being expectant fathers.

"Darling, look at this, there's a lovely house for sale that could be perfect for us."
"Let me see," and looking at the book Elizabeth said, "it looks lovely, where is it."
"Phillimore Place. It even has a basement cinema, should we buy it?"
"Should we?"
"Shall we?"

About the Author

This is the debut novel by Martin Lesley. He is retired and lives in Hertfordshire with his wife. He has two grown up children who have flown the nest, spends as much time as possible on the golf course, but has decided that he would publish this story, dreamt of more than twenty years ago, hoping that readers would enjoy it.

Printed in Great Britain
by Amazon